THESE ARE MY CHILDREN

SELECT KATHA TITLES

KATHA SHORT FICTION
Asomiya Handpicked Fictions
Basheer Fictions
Bhupen Khakhar Maganbhai's Glue ...
Black Margins
By Sa'adat Hasan Manto
Ed Muhammad Umar Memon
Downfall by Degrees
By Abdullah Hussein
Forsaking Paradise:
Stories from Ladakh
Hindi Handpicked Fictions
Home and Away
By Ramachandra Sharma
I am Madhabi
By Suchitra Bhattacharyya
Inspector Matadeen on the Moon
By Harishankar Parsai
Katha Prize Stories 13
Ed Geeta Dharmarajan
Masti Fictions
Mauni Fictions
New Urdu Fictions
Selected by Joginder Paul
One Last Story and That's It
By Etgar Keret
Paul Zacharia Two Novellas
Pudumaippittan Fictions
Raja Rao Fictions
Separate Journeys
Ed Geeta Dharmarajan
20 Stories from South Asia
The End of Human History
By Hasan Manzar
The Heart of the Matter
Stories from the Northeast
The Resthouse
By Ahmad Nadeem Qasimi
Two Novellas and a Story
By Ambai
Uday Prakash
Short Shorts Long Shots
Waterness
By Na Muthuswamy

KATHA NOVELS
Arumugam
By Imayam
Atonement and The Stone Laughs
By LaSaRa
JJ: Some Jottings
By SuRaa
Listen Girl!
By Krishna Sobti
Over to you, Kadambari
By Alka Saraogi
Padmavati
By A Madhaviah
Remembering Amma
Thi Jaa
Seven Sixes are Forty Three
By Kiran Nagarkar
Singarevva and the Palace
By Chandrasekhar Kambar
The Heart has its Reasons
By Krishna Sobti
The Life and Times of Pratapa Mudaliar
By Mayuram Vedanayakam Pillai
The Survivors
By Gurdial Singh

SCREENPLAY
The Master Carpenter
By MT Vasudevan Nair

POETRY
Seeking the Beloved
Poetry of Shah Abdul Latif
Tamil New Poetry
Translated by K S Subramanian

NON-FICTION
A Child Widow's Story
By Monica Felton
Ismat: Her Life, Her Times
Ed Sukrita Paul Kumar
Links in the Chain
By Mahadevi Varma
Rajaji
By Monica Felton
Storytellers at Work
Travel Writing and the Empire
Ed Sachidananda Mohanty
The Epic of Pabuji
By John D Smith
Upendranath Ashk
By Daisy Rockwell

ALT (APPROACHES TO LITERATURES IN TRANSLATION)
Translating Caste
Ed Tapan Basu
Translating Desire
Ed Brinda Bose
Translating Partition
Ed Ravikant & Tarun K Saint

THESE ARE MY CHILDREN

DAMODAR MAUZO

Translated from the Konkani
by Xavier Cota

First published by Katha in 2007

KATHA
A3, Sarvodaya Enclave
Sri Aurobindo Marg, New Delhi 110 017

Phone: (91-11) 4141 6600, 4141 6610

Fax: (91-11) 2651 4373

E-mail: marketing@katha.org

Website: http://www.katha.org

KATHA is a registered nonprofit organization
devoted to enhancing the joy of reading.
KATHA VILASAM is its story research and resource centre.

Cover Design: Geeta Dharmarajan

Cover Painting: S P Chendvanker

Line Drawings: Rizio Yohannan Raj

Typeset in 11 on 16pt Agaramond at Katha

Katha regularly plants trees to replace the wood used in the making of its books.

ISBN 978-81-89020-99-6

First Reprint 2012, Second Reprint 2016

Contents

The Vow

Summer had just begun. I was posted as a curate at Majorda Church. Almost a month went by in acquainting myself with the church routine, meeting the parishioners and sorting out pending matters at the attached chapels.

The priestly vocation suits me fine. Befriending people, playing with children, encouraging students, visiting the sick, helping the needy – these things came naturally to me even as a layman. They had now become my duties, and I applied myself to my tasks with renewed vigour.

Once, I delivered a moving sermon about how a woman once lost her child at a fair and how the child was found some years later after the mother had made a vow to Our Lady. The congregation was impressed. After Mass, everyone left, save one old man who was still on his knees, deep in meditation. Not wanting to disturb him, I went in silently. After a word with the Vicar, I gave some instructions to the sacristan, changed my vestments and came out.

The old man was standing in the church doorway. He must have been around fifty-five but his emaciated frame and wrinkled skin gave him the appearance of a seventy year old. A kabay hung from his shoulders. This loose full-length gown worn by elderly working class Christian Goan men in the past is hardly seen nowadays. That's why I found it a little odd. I'm not a face-reader, but at first glance, he appeared to be a kind man.

He seemed to have been waiting for me, and bowed in greeting. I may be a priest, but I am young too, and feel discomfited when elderly folk bow down to me. However, you cannot explain this to them because they tend to take offence. I went close to him, patted him on the shoulder and said, "Hello Pai, how are you?"

I had barely uttered these words when the old man's lips began to quiver. He stared at me, tears welling up in his eyes. With trembling hands, he felt my hand on his shoulder. "My son! You are my son?"

I replied, not missing a beat, "Even though you did not beget me, you may consider me your son."

My words broke his stupor. Wiping his eyes on the sleeve of his kabay, he apologized. "I'm sorry, Father. You called me Pai and I thought I had found my son! He must be as old as you –"

I understood his grief. His son had gone far away. A sailor perhaps. "Where is your boy?"

Shaking his head, he stifled a sob. "I don't know! Nobody knows." His gaze travelled upwards and his fingers pointed at the cross. "He alone knows."

I looked at him in consternation. A fleeting doubt crossed my mind. Was this elderly man a little unstable of mind? His dishevelled state troubled me.

"What's your name?" I asked.

"Camil."

"Where do you live?"

"Beyond the lake, in the house with a balcao."

"Camil-bab, go home now. I'll see you later," I said.

"Father Curate! I too will make the vow you spoke about in your sermon!" Camil said, looking intently at my face, awaiting my response. I turned away and said nothing.

"If I do, my son will come back home. Won't he?" he pleaded.

"Trust in God and look for him." I said, patting his back.

Camil turned and started for home, but his parting words kept ringing in my ears. "I have looked for him everywhere, Father. I'm still looking for him. And I will keep on looking."

I had no inclination to go on. With leaden feet, I went back into the church. "Tell me something," I called out to the sacristan. "Who was that old man, the last person praying here? Do you know him?"

"Who? Camil?"

"Yes. What's his story? Where's his son?" I was anxious to know.

"It's a sad story, Father Curate. I know Camil well. An excellent man. A friend in need. He has no one now and lives alone, poor chap. His wife died in childbirth, leaving Camil to bring up their only son on his own. One day, when he was about twelve, the boy just disappeared. No one knows where he went. They searched everywhere for him. This happened about twenty years ago, and till date, there has been no news about him. Nobody even knows whether he's dead or alive."

"And Camil's still hoping to find him?" I asked in surprise.

"Yes, he thinks he will come back. Every day he looks for him with a lot of hope. He's old now and sometimes acts slightly crazy. It's a long story. When his son disappeared, Camil searched frantically for him. He even went to Bombay to look for him. He still asks all the tarvottis if they have come across his son on their ship or in any foreign port. Poor man. A very decent sort. During the last ten years or so, Camil even adopted four or five young boys. But they all cheated him and ran away."

"What's that? Why did he adopt them? And five too?"

"Five of them, but not all at once - one at a time. Why he adopted them of course, he alone knows. He may have felt that the money and care he lavished on some child he

adopted would somehow reach his son. The boys were all rascals, though. They feasted well at Camil's expense and abandoned him in the end."

I felt my chest constrict on hearing Camil's sad story.

The day crept by. I didn't see Camil at church the following day, and cycled to his home that afternoon. Camil was lying down in the balcao, still wearing the same kabay. Seeeing me he got up quickly.

"Who? My son's back? Come Jose, come!"

I had thought that Camil had risen in deference to the Father Curate, but it seemed that he had mistaken me for his long lost son, despite my cassock. "Camil-bab, I am not Jose," I said gently. "I am the priest, Padre-Cura."

Camil's disappointment was palpable. He sat down limply in the balcao. By this time, a neighbour had come up to me. "He's not well, Father. If anybody comes to visit, he rejoices, saying, Jose has come! Then slumps down in disappointment."

I was moved. I went over to Camil's side. "Camil-bab, you didn't come to Church today?"

"I cannot manage to go every day, Pad' Cur. I came yesterday and I'm still in bed today."

"Don't worry. God is with you even at home, to His poor and the distressed people."

Camil nodded. "I have made a vow to Our Lady," he said, after a pause.

"Good." He expected me to go on and say that his son would come back now. But I could not bring myself to say it.

"Now my Jose will come. He will." Camil muttered to himself.

After that day, I didn't go to Camil's house. I was afraid that he would confront me and demand why his son hadn't been brought back to him despite his vow. Trust in God and look for him, I had told him earlier. What could I answer if he should ask me, "How long am I to look for him?"

I might not have visited him afterwards, but I continued to enquire about him. Camil's health was failing. His mind wandered. But the deep conviction that his son would come back, kept growing in him.

The monsoons were approaching. Schools had reopened after the summer break.

One day, a widow from Chandor came with her child to the church. Driven by poverty, the woman wanted to keep her child in the parish boarding. "Father, it would be a great favour to me if you could keep him in your boarding. He will do whatever work you give him." There were other such poor boarders with us; I agreed to keep her child and sent the woman home.

I called the boy to me, a smart fourteen year old. "What's your name, son?"

"Jose." As soon as I heard the name, I recalled Camil and his son, and an idea occurred to me. Camil was already slightly senile; to him, any person would be his son. If this boy were sent to Camil's place as his son, it might just work. It would be like lighting two candles with one flame – the boy would gain a guardian and Camil, a young companion in his old age.

I grew restless once the idea occurred to me. I took the youngster into confidence and taught him to call Camil "Pai" and shortly after, we went to Camil's house. It was evening when we reached. Camil was stoking the kitchen fire.

"Camil-bab, look who's come!" I called out from outside. The old man straightened up quickly. Wiping his hands on his kabay, he asked, "Who's come?"

"It's Jose! Look here," and I prodded the boy forward. As instructed, Jose called out, "Pai!"

"My son ... my son has come," muttered Camil as he shuffled forward.

The balcao was lit by the weak rays of the dying sun. Camil examined Jose, and then turned to me disbelievingly. "Who, Father? Who says this is my Jose? Don't fool me! My Jose must be a grown man today. As grown up as you."

And with that, he sank down. Not quite as senile as I had thought.

"Perhaps I won't be able to recognize Jose. He must be older now, but he will recognize me. Do you know why I still wear this kabay? People tell me to stop wearing it. Let them say what they want. When my Jose went away, I was wearing a kabay. If Jose comes back, he will recognize me at least by my kabay, wouldn't he? He'll know my kabay ..." The long speech had exhausted him. I didn't know what to say. We fell silent.

"Father Curate," he said at last. "My Jose will come. I have reposed my faith in Our Lady. I will keep looking for him. Jose will come, and I will not die till he comes. I will not die!" He began to sob.

I felt humbled, but not because of my failed attempt but by Camil's intense faith in God. For a moment, even I was swept off by the intensity of his belief – surely Jose would come!

With the boy in tow, I returned home with heavy steps.

About a fortnight passed. Suddenly, one evening, Camil's neighbour came rushing up to me. "Father, Camil is dying! Come soon and administer the last sacrament."

"Dying? Which doctor said so?"

"No doctor, but I doubt if he'll pull through this time."

The woman's words angered me. These people first think of calling the priest, not the doctor!

"Bring the doctor, first. Tell him that I have sent for him. I'll come soon."

The neighbour left. For a moment I was paralyzed. Camil is dying! His words – "I will not die till Jose comes!" – still rang in my ears. Poor Camil. Death was at his doorstep, but hope still stayed alive.

Putting away my work, I set off hurriedly. The Angelus bells rang as I reached Camil's house. The doctor, who was about to leave after examining his patient, stopped to speak to me. "Old age. He's gone weak. In the grip of a strong fever too. I have injected an antibiotic, but it would be better if you gave him Extreme Unction, Father." He left, while I still stood on the patio. The neighbour looked at me from the doorway.

"Is he asleep?" I asked.

"No, Father. He's awake. He keeps asking for his son."

"You can go now. Come back after your supper. I'll stay

with him awhile." I waited until the neighbour had gone.

Dusk had set in. A small kerosene lamp flickered in the room. Camil lay on an old cot.

I cast a swift glance all around. The pervading gloom covered everything like a blanket. I couldn't see anyone. Hurriedly, I took off my cassock and flung it on an armchair. I entered in my trousers and shirt.

"Pai!" I called out softly.

Camil was awake. Even his eyes were open. My call reached his ears. He opened his eyes wide to see who it was.

"Pai, it's Jose. I have come." I edged closer to the cot.

Camil struggled to get up. "My son – " he murmured. "Jose? My son, Jose? My son! My son!" Overjoyed, Camil could utter no other words.

Suddenly, Camil sat up as if he had found some hidden strength.

"Pail" I buried my face in Camil's shoulder. Seeing Camil's emotion, even my eyes filled up. Nothing could contain the tears that coursed down our faces. There was no fear of Camil recognizing me in the dim light of that kerosene lamp. I hugged Camil tight. He ran his fingers down my back. His body was burning with fever, but his face was aglow.

"Go to sleep now, Pai." I said, but Camil wouldn't move.

"You came," he whispered. "I knew it. You made it just in time." His voice was rasping. "I made a vow to Our Lady. Father Curate knows about it. I had faith in God. That's why you came – now – now I cannot. You fulfill my vow. You ... " Camil's voice drifted.

His head slumped on my shoulder. His limbs relaxed. Very gently, I lowered his head onto the pillow. Camil's eyes were open. With a touch, I closed them, and covered his body with a sheet.

Stepping out of the room, I donned my cassock again.

Minguel's Kin

Minguel was on his way home from Mass when he heard the kogull's distinctive cry. "Coo-oo, coo-oo." It looks like she's followed me here too, murmured Minguel. Then he smiled to himself. As if there's only one cuckoo in the world!

"Hi there, Mingloo!" Roque Saman was passing by. "What are you smiling at? Received a parcel from your son? Or are you thinking of your daughter?" And he walked on without waiting for a reply.

Minguel smiled wryly. Roque Santan was a friend from childhood days. Why couldn't the man have stopped and chatted a bit? All he did was make snide remarks about his son and daughter before walking away. He had had a lucky escape, because in the course of exchanging some gossip, Minguel would certainly have pulled out some skeletons from Roque San tan's closet. Perhaps, that was why Roque had quickly walked on!

When Minguel reached his doorstep, the crows set off a loud cawing.

"Hold on, hold on !" he said. "Am I that late? I have come back at the usual time. You guys have no patience." Minguel darted inside. Emerging with the rice that he had saved from last night's supper, he called out to the crows. What a racket! As two dozen crows pounced on the cooked rice, they pecked at one another, forcing Minguel to admonish them, "How many times do I have to tell you? Stop squabbling! If you want more, I'll give you more. Eat in peace, you gluttons!"

When, at last, he wiped the pan clean and threw the last grains to them, the crows were almost eating out of his hands. Minguel sat on the steps, watching the last grain being picked. The din died down. The last crow flew away, and Minguel went inside.

"Have your guests gone?" asked Feliza as she poured his tea.

"They are not guests! Those who come every day aren't called that, they are family. And the real family have become guests!" said Minguel as he washed his hands and took the cup of tea.

"You call them guests? In the last four years, neither Victor nor Lucy has bothered to come to see us. They don't even know whether their parents are dead or alive. How could our own children turn so ungrateful?" Feliza remarked bitterly as she sipped her tea.

"And you want me to take some of our mangoes to Victor! Our new graft gave just about ninety mangoes. Your first thought was Victor. I for one, will not take them to him! It seems that he's bought a car – a tourist taxi. But did he even think of taking his parents for a drive to Colva beach?"

Feliza finished her tea. "Okay, that's enough. But wasn't it you who insisted on sending mangad to Lucy last year? Or have you forgotten?"

Minguel hadn't forgotten. He had sent the mango jam with Custodio when the seaman was going to Mumbai to join ship. Lucy had not even bothered to acknowledge it. A couple of months later though, Custodio had written from across the seas that Lucy had told him to keep the jar, and that he and his crew-mates had really relished the mangad.

Luciana had been her parents' favourite. Minguel had only done his segundo grau at the Portuguese primary school. When Lucy passed SSCE, the High School Examination, Minguel's joy knew no bounds. He sent her to coqege. When she graduated with a BA degree, Minguel was on cloud nine. Lucy then told him, "Pai, Goa now has a university. I want to do my Master's degree." Minguel was only too happy to give his consent. Victor was then in the

Highet Secondary, and Minguel's salary was under severe strain. But he took it in his stride.

Before the completion of her first year of post-graduation at the university, Lucy confided to her parents, "Pai, Mai, I have a close friend. We want to get married."

Minguel and Feliza were stunned. What about her studies? Who was the boy? Not to mention the enormous expenses which a wedding entailed!

Charlie Abraham was from a well-to-do family from Mumbai. He had completed his post-graduation in Management Studies from Goa University. His family owned a thriving export business, and they had a beautiful bungalow in the posh Pedder Road locality.

Minguel was a little disappointed because Charlie wasn't a Goan, but he swallowed his objections with the consolation that Lucy would be comfortably married into an affluent family.

One day, Charlie's Mama and Papa came to visit them in a Mercedes Benz. They didn't exactly hold kerchiefs to their noses, but the house clearly didn't meet with their approval. It was their last visit as well.

Bowled over as they were by Charlie's family's wealth, Minguel and Feliza felt overwhelmed and apprehensive. They were relieved when Charlie's parents pronounced their approval of Lucy, and that they shouldn't worry about either dowry or the wedding expenses. They bade a tearful farewell to their Lucy after a civil marriage in Goa. Minguel and Feliza didn't go to Mumbai for the wedding, but they satisfied themselves listening to an account of the

grand reception from Gomes Bhatkar, the landlord's son who was in a senior position with the Times of India. After the wedding, Lucy had written just one letter. Later, when Minguel longed to see his daughter and announced that he was making plans to go to Mumbai to see her, they got a message – "You needn't come. We're all coming down to Goa in December, during the Exposition of the relics of Sr. Francis Xavier in Old Goa."

How happy Minguel and Feliza were!

As planned, the entire family came down. They stayed in a five-star hotel. Lucy finally came to her parental home, alone. She seemed distant, almost like a stranger. She concurred only when asked if there was any good news.

And when she was solicitously queried about any duvalle or pregnancy cravings that her mother could satisfy, she only laughed. "What can you give me, Mai? I lack nothing. Tell me if you need anything!"

After that, they received a letter that she had given birth to a baby boy. And that too, three months after the delivery. Baba must now be seven years old. They had heard that she had had a baby girl, a few years later. But –

Feliza cursed,"Damn it! I'm getting so forgetful! I poured out the milk and left it down." She lifted the aluminium bowl, climbed onto the stool and placed it on the wall. Of late, this squirrel had developed a taste for milk, and would scamper up and make a peremptory demand every day. A coconut sapling grew behind their wall. Squirrels would clamber onto its fronds and over the tiles, even onto the rafters. Recently, a squirrel had slipped and fallen to the ground. Stunned, it had lain motionless, as though dead. Feliza had tried to revive it quickly, by sprinkling water on it with her fingers. She had put some milk in the same bowl she held now, and kept it in front of the squirrel. When it recovered consciousness, Feliza stepped back.

The squirrel was timid at first. But gradually, it started sipping the milk. Afterwards, though, it was quite amusing. It could not climb up the wall, and started running about the house, darting hither and tither. Feliza brought a rafter and leaned it against the wall. The squirrel quickly climbed on it, and was gone in a moment. From then on, at teatime, Feliza would pour some milk into the bowl, climb onto the stool and keep it on the wall. Of late, a couple of baby squirrels had started accompanying her.

"This mother has passed on her craze to her kids," said Feliza.

"Craze for what? For milk or you?" quipped Minguel, making Feliza feel as if a peacock feather had caressed her heart.

Putting down his teacup, Minguel got up and went to check the mangoes that had been kept for ripening. "These mangoes should ripen by tomorrow. I think we should sell off fifty mangoes. What do you think?"

"Why only fifty? Let's sell them all. Who's going to eat so many mangoes?" Feliza wanted to know.

"But you love them! Let's keep at least twenty five."

"Keep five, if you must. Four for us and one for the squirrel," said Feliza.

"Fine. I'll take them tomorrow morning to Vasco. They say you get a fair price there. I'll go by the first train. I hope to get a good price." Minguel got up. "I'll be able to buy the provisions."

"Aren't you going to buy fish now?" Feliza reminded him.

"Forget it. Isn't there some dried fish? Make a curry out of it."

Normally, Minguel enjoyed going to the market and gossiping a little. Of late, though, people had begun to avoid him. Earlier, feni worth ·a couple of rupees would buy him company ready to listen to him for an hour. But everybody seemed to be avoiding him ever since Minguel's purse strings had tightened, and he had stopped going to bars and pubs.

Not that he had totally given up on life. Whenever he sold his coconuts and had some spare cash, he would take a nip of liquor home. And when he felt really lonely, he would take a small swig, go to the backyard, and talk endlessly to the mynah sitting on the custard-apple tree, or to the cuckoo hiding in the thick-set mango leaves. And it didn't matter if he failed to find them, because even a lowly crow would do.

Behind the house a hen's coop stood on one side, and a cowshed on the other. They had sold off the cattle about seven or eight years ago when the work became too much for Feliza, and though she insisted that he dismantle the shed, Minguel wouldn't hear of it. Recent times had seen a lot of migrant ghantis arrive, who were prepared to pay even a hundred rupees as rent for accommodation in such sheds. Tomorrow, if anything were to happen to me, Feliza shouldn't be totally abandoned, he thought. The rent will give her some income, and she'll have some company too.

When he expressed these thoughts to her one day, she flared up. "As if it's time for you to be thinking of your death!" By evening, when the Angelus bell rang at aimori, she had cooled down. "You weren't wrong, Mingloo. Tomorrow, when I'm dead, it will be good for you to have some neighbours. We'll thatch that hut."

They had done so with coconut palm fronds just the other day. Discovering that it was very pleasant there in the evenings with the gentle breeze blowing in, Minguel had taken his easy chair to the hut. These days, he had replaced his penchant for the fish market with a walk to the hut-shed.

"Coo-ooo!" The cuckoo's call greeted him.

He had been hearing the same call for the last four years. In the beginning, he would imagine that it was Lucy calling out to him. Perhaps she was thinking of home. When she had been a child, Minguel would bring her bhajjias from Babu's cart, unfailingly. Lucy loved them. That used to irritate Victor. So Minguel would occasionally bring Victor's favourite patties too. But Minguel preferred buying bhajjias, perhaps because patties were comparatively expensive .

He drew in his breath inadvertently and could almost inhale the aroma of the steaming gram-flour fritters in his nostrils!

"Coo-ooo!"

Lucy must be thinking of us. Lucy too had a sweet voice, just like the cuckoo. When she sang in the church choir, her soaring voice would rise sweetly, above the rest.

Minguel had been very fond of the cuckoo at first, but just the other day, Joslyn, who was studying zoology in college, had told him that the singing cuckoo wasn't a female but a male, in which case – was this Victor? Does he remember those patties, I wonder? It must be Victor. That's why he doesn't show his face, and calls out from afar.

Musing thus, Minguel reached the guava tree. This tree was beyond the hut. Minguel used to chase away the children who stoned the tree to knock down guavas. But last year, he had spied a couple of parakeets on the top of the tree. The ripe guavas on the tree had been pecked. The sight filled Minguel with immense joy. He suddenly had an idea. He had scraped two cotties clean. Last year, after the monsoons had withdrawn, he had placed those coconut shells in a fork of the guava tree. Every morning, before going for Mass, he would put rice grains in one and millet in the other. By evening, both the shells would have been picked clean.

A bulbul flew away as Minguel approached it, now. But the mynah on the top branch stayed where it was, near the coconut shell. Shading his eyes from the sun with his hands, Minguel looked up towards the mynah, only to find that the bird had swivelled its head to look at him. It stared at him quizzically for a brief moment, and then, flew off.

Minguel looked with interest. There were still some

grains in both the coconut shell bowls. He chided himself, worried that the mynah might have flown away hungry because he had lifted his hand to shade himself. Gently retracing his steps, he moved his easy-chair to a shady spot outside the hut, and sat down.

This mynah was certainly better than that cuckoo, he decided. It simply didn't know the meaning of fear. He recalled that it would come quite close and pick up twigs, when they were thatching the hut. And she had quite coolly filched at least twenty straws from the hay he had kept for ripening the mangoes, from right under his nose. Feliza's explanation was that she was probably building a nest. She wouldn't flyaway even when Minguel was quite close by, and would hop around him like a tame bird. Minguel had started doling out extra grains into the bowls just for her.

In fact, just the other day, Feliza had begun to complain, "Fistfuls of grain every day add up to quite a few kilos by the end of the month. We'd better stop this!"

That had irritated Minguel. "Have you ever wondered how much food Victor and Lucy would need, if they were home? Have you seen how many birds come to feed here?" And he proudly added, "Feliza, did you see how the mynah and even those other birds don't fly off when I go near them?"

But Victor had gone away, never to return. He should have been born to a rich man. Not to Minguel, who had never known riches. Who was the only son of a poor tailor, and had studied in the Portuguese Primary School and after

struggling through his segundo grau, had dropped out after a couple of chisses in the English High School.

By pulling some strings, he had managed to get a job in the government as a peon. He had retired thirty years later as a lower division clerk with about forty thousand rupees as his terminal benefits, including his provident fund. It was the first time he had seen so much money together.

But he still had a few obligations. Lucy was already married, so that was one worry less. However, the house was in urgent need of repairs and was threatening to come down. He had taken a loan to purchase the land on which his house stood and a bit around it from his landlord the bhatkar, and now, he owned the title to it. After deducting the balance of the loan, he had received forty thousand rupees. This was all he had, to manage the rebuilding of the adobe wall and the pillar of the balcao which was tilting, the work of the small plot surrounding the house and Victor's education. Most importantly, he had to provide for his own future and his wife's as well.

Although he had retired, Minguel was still quite physically active. So, just as he was thinking of taking up another job, Victor had sprung a surprise on him.

"Pai, I have been thinking – I want to set up a shack on the beach. It's a good business, especially now, with so many foreign tourists coming to Goa."

Minguel surveyed Victor's excited face, surprised. Was he asking him or telling him?

"But Victor, you haven't finished college!"

"Pai, it's better to start business right away, instead of wasting time in college. Wouldn't it be better to make my own way instead of wandering around aimlessly, looking for a job after B Com?"

"Don't get carried away –"

"I'm not, Pai. I have been offered a shack on lease. I may not get another chance like this." Excitement rose in Victor's voice.

"Where will you get the money?" Minguel asked casually.

"You have it, don't you? What are you going to do with the money, in any case? Deposit it in the bank at ten per cent interest?· Give it to me instead. I'll double it in two years and return it to you."

Minguel was stunned into silence. A shack! Benjamin's son has put up a shack, and was selling drugs there. Just the other day, Benjamin was saying with tears in his eyes that soon after his son began to peddle drugs, he had become addicted as well! Minguel's worry for Victor deepened.

"Don't get involved in the shack business, my son," Minguel tried to make him understand. "It hasn't done anyone any good."

Victor's initial surprise gave way to anger as he fumed, "Who told you that? People have earned thousands in the shack business. They're queuing up at the village panchayat for shack licences, and you claim that nobody has prospered in this line?"

Here was a quandary. There were the house repairs, work in the property, ailments in old age – and Victor, stubbornly standing his ground. Minguel consulted Feliza and conveyed his decision.

On hearing his father turn down his request, Victor flew into a mad rage. "Eat your money! I don't want even a paisa of it. Other parents even sell off their property to help their children. And here, you have the money, but won't part with it. What do you think? Do you imagine that I won't go ahead if you don't give me the money? You'll see! I won't rest until I buy that shack. I don't want your alms or sympathy. From today – no, from this very moment, I'm leaving this house. I shall never step in here again!"

And without heeding his mother's entreaties, Victor packed his things and stormed out, leaving behind a yawning emptiness. Minguel sensed a hollowness gnawing at the pit of his stomach. Victor was gone forever, breaking the bonds of affection that had tied them together.

When, after two days of anxiously searching for him, Victor had still not returned, Minguel grew angry. He went around telling all and sundry that his son had become a vagabond, that he wouldn't listen to his father, and had fallen into bad company. And how he had tried to dissuade him in vain. Half a nip of feni in the morning, and half a nip in the evening, and he would go on and on, like a needle stuck in the same groove. He lacked no listeners too, for Minguel footed the bill of all those who wanted their throats slaked.

After three or four months of this sorry routine, Feliza stepped in. She began to bring the liquor home and commenced the house repairs. Minguel too lent a hand. Later, he started working on the trees in the coconut grove, upturning the soil, fertilizing the trees. The routine of work left him no time for brooding or gossiping.

News of his son had started dribbling in. He had set up a shack on the beach. It was doing pretty well. Cooks had been brought from Punjab. The shack was crowded at night.

The reports left him with mixed feelings. He was pleased that Victor was prospering, but he was irritated as well. Honest people shouldn't get mixed up with running shacks. Shacks were into drug peddling. Victor must be involved in drugs too. He would get caught some day and then he would have to face the music. If that ever happened, Minguel decided that he would hire the best lawyer and bail him out. Then Victor would not involve himself with shacks anymore.

Victor had bought a motorbike. Within a year, he had taken up a small hotel on lease at Colva. Two boys from the village had started working for him in the hotel. His son had bought a tourist taxi. It seemed, he had opened a business account in a bank in Margao too. News reached constantly. Minguel was pleased to hear of his son's rising prosperity. But doubts lingered. There must be a drug connection or maybe he has taken a huge loan from the bank.

One thing that did change was that Minguel stopped talking to people about his son. For the people had started telling Minguel about Victor instead.

Was it Victor's fault or mine? The question continued to haunt Minguel. Desperate to find an answer, he pestered Feliza. The day he insisted that he had been right, Feliza would declare that they should have listened to their son, and that the fault was hers. And on the days he kicked himself for not having been more understanding, Feliza would point out how their son had erred.

Minguel suffered a twinge of envy as he caught sight of Manuel Bhatkar, proudly riding in his lawyer son's Maruti car. Then, thankfully, he recalled the fate of Joao who had trustingly transferred his estate to his son, only to be dumped into the Asilo, the Home for the Aged, and heaved a sigh of relief.

Let bygones be bygones, he thought. He was anxious for a reconciliation with his son. Victor really must come back home. He had even tried to obliquely convey the message to Victor. But his son did not respond. He visited the village, but never met them; attended the annual village feast, and even made it a point to lunch with the president of the feast committee – but wasn't concerned in the least about his parents. He never even inquired about them.

Deep in a maze of memories, Minguel was faintly conscious that somebody was calling out to him, "Hi there Mingloo!"

"Sounds like Salvador," Minguel murmured, hurriedly rising from the easy-chair. The chair that he had placed in the shade was now in the sun. How had he been so oblivious of it? His back felt quite stiff; he must have sat in the same position for a long time. By the time he had started limping towards the house with his hand on his painful hip, Feliza had come to the back door.

"Are you deaf? Or were you asleep? That Salu's been calling out to you for ages!"

"I'm coming. I just heard him. Oh, my back ..." muttered Minguel, shuffling to the front door.

Salu was sitting on the balcao wearing an ill-fitting pair of shorts, puffing away on a bidi. An old hat sitting askew on his head completed the picture of a comic character from the teatro. But since this was how he always looked, his whacky appearance evoked no amusement.

"You never come even when you're called, so what brings you this way today?" Minguel's greeting was a trifle acerbic.

"Don't I come when you call? Don't talk rubbish. I couldn't come last year when you called, because I was ill." Salu flicked away his bidi. "I was laid up in the house for twenty days after my fall from the jackfruit tree! Did you even come by to ask after my health at that time?" He lobbed the ball back into Minguel's court.

"Oh, alright." Minguel came back to the point. "Why have you come now?"

"Mahadeo told me, so I ..."

"Told you what?"

"It seems that he had come to pluck your mangoes the other day. He told me that one of your coconut trees had lost its crown and was dead."

"That's right. What a superb tree it was! It was affected by muddoll. I just didn't notice the stem-rot. It used to

yield at least fifty coconuts at each harvest. We got the last yield last March. By the time we noticed that the coconuts were falling, it had started shedding leaves and tender nuts, and soon became a skeleton." Minguel was almost talking to himself. "God knows who cast his evil eye on it."

"You know, one can make good money from rafters, now. Once the rains have gone over it, nobody will take it even for free. I'll take it if you are ready to sell it."

The tree rose upright before Minguel's eyes, stark and bereft of its crown. Salu wasn't wrong, of course. It was dead. And there was the fear that it could fall and cause further damage in a storm.

"See Mingloo, I require longish logs. I had a look at your tree – it's good. I'll take it for a hundred rupees." Salu was brisk and business-like.

"What does a hundred rupees get nowadays, Salu?" Minguel began to bargain. "You can get two long logs, each of which will yield at least five rafters. One hundred and fifty, take it or leave it."

"Forget it," Salu promptly got up. "Rafters are there in plenty, but I need two beams, which is why I'm looking for trees. But a hundred and fifty is too much. Remedios offered to sell his for a hundred."

The hundred rupees gleamed before his eyes. In a flash, Minguel realized this month's provisions would be taken care of. "Wait Salu," he shouted. "I wouldn't dream of depriving you and selling it to somebody else. You can take it."

Salu promptly fished out a fifty-rupee note from his pocket. Putting it in Minguel's hands, he said, "Here's the advance. I'll pay the balance when I've felled the tree. I'll come tomorrow with the woodcutters."

"Not tomorrow. I have to go to Vasco. Would the day after be alright?" Minguel asked solicitously.

Slightly puzzled, Salu nodded. "Okay, okay. The day after tomorrow then. But don't postpone it further."

"Come any time the day after. It's fixed." Minguel stood rooted to the spot until Salu had disappeared. Today wasn't too bad.

After returning from church the next day, he cleaned out the rice from the earthen pot and scattered it for the cawing crows milling around. Without waiting to gossip with them, he went back inside. The mangoes had ripened well. A few more days, and they would have been over-ripe. Selecting about twenty mangoes for Feliza, he counted the rest. Sixty nine. With a heavy heart, he selected six smaller mangoes from those that he had kept aside, and rounded the figure to seventy five. Drinking up the tea Feliza had poured out for him, he hurried out of the house.

By the time he reached Vasco, the sun was blazing overhead. The train was late. Worried that it would take a long time to sell his mangoes, he hurried to leave when he was suddenly accosted by the stationmaster. Quickly, he fished out his ticket, but the stationmaster seemed more interested in the price of the mangoes in Minguel's bag.

This was rather confusing. He wondered what the price

of musrad mangoes was in Vasco. In the village tinto, he would have got thirty rupees for a dozen, but in Vasco –

"Fifty rupees a dozen. Five rupees less for you, sir!"

"Fifty rupees? Nobody will take them for even forty! Be reasonable!" countered the stationmaster.

Last night, Feliza had reckoned that if all were sold, they should get at least two hundred rupees.

By this time, two more potential customers had sidled to the basket and were appraising the mangoes. The stationmaster wasn't amused.

"How much are they?" asked one customer.

By way of turning him away, Minguel said, "Fifty rupees a dozen, sir."

"I hope they're good!" said the second man.

"I'll take a dozen," said the first, pulling out a bag from his pocket.

"I've bought the lot," announced the stationmaster, dragging both Minguel and his bag into his office. "At forty five rupees right?" He said, as he counted them out. "Six dozen comes to two hundred and seventy rupees and the balance is bonus, okay?"

Minguel might have got a better price in the market, but this wasn't a bad deal either, and with minimum effort too. He caught the returning train, and was home by noon.

Feliza had already had her lunch. She quickly served Minguel his.

After lunch, Minguel cut open one of the mangoes reserved for Feliza. She took the first sliver and kept it on the wall for the squirrel.

Minguel unrolled his mat and lay down to rest, happy that he did not have to forego his afternoon siesta. When he awoke, the sun was about to set. He took a long draught of cool water from the earthen gurgulet. Gathering the hay used for ripening the mangoes, Minguel threw it in the cowshed. The moment he was out of the house, the mynah flew past him, whirring its wings, and alighted on the guava tree.

God! In the rush of going to Vasco, he had forgotten to fill up grains in the bowls. Minguel went inside hurriedly, and found the paddy container empty. Putting his hand in the ration rice tin, he found that it too, was almost empty. Resolving to buy some rice next day, he drew out two fistfuls of rice and millet each, and filled the two coconut shell bowls.

As Minguel stood there, the mynah darted in. Dipping its yellow-tipped beak into the bowl, it pecked at the grains and without waiting to swallow, flapped its wings and flew away.

"Co-ooo ...!"

Minguel's glance rose to the mango tree. Damn the blighter! That cuckoo never shows himself. I wonder if he'll come and eat the grains when my back is turned at least. Doesn't he ever get hungry? Or does he get enough outside? Why's he calling, then? And he's still hiding. He must be on one of the mango branches.

Sinking into the easy-chair, Minguel called out loudly, "Why are you hiding? Come in front of me. Scared that I'll gobble you up? I won't even touch you. Let me see you just once!"

Hearing Minguel's entreaties, Feliza laughed with derision; she had come to the back door with the swill for the pigs. "This man's own children don't come to him, why would the birds come?"

Minguel flared up. "And you? As if you could handle them! It's you who spoilt them! My birds are far better." Muttering, he went straight back into the house, removed a two rupee note from the trousers he had worn to Vasco, and stuffed it into his shirt pocket.

"Yo-yo, baa-baa!" Feliza was calling out to the pigs and hens. Raising his voice above the din, he told her tersely, "I'm going to the market. I'll hang around the tinto for a while."

Well aware that once he had stormed out of the house in a huff, he would invariably land up at Inacio's pub, Feliza kept up a constant tirade of curses at him until he returned.

Salu called out to him the next morning just as Minguel was having his breakfast, having fed the crows after returning from Mass. Two labouters had accompanied him. Minguel finished his tea, rinsed out his cup in a hurry, and slipped on his sandals.

"Don't bother, my men will cut the tree! They won't finish making the rafters and beams today," Salu remarked.

"No problem," shrugged Minguel. 'I'll just come along. I don't have anything to do at home." They walked from the back door into the coconut grove.

"What a superb tree," remarked a logger. "Definitely six rafters from the lower log and five from the top one – nothing less than ten hands each!"

Salu wasn't too pleased about this conversation happening in Minguel's presence. His expression reminded Minguel of the irritated look on the stationmaster's face, when the other customers had started showing interest in his mangoes.

"We'll discuss about that later," said Salu brusquely. "I want a beam of twelve hands from the lower half and rafters from the top log. Rocky, you climb the tree and cut off the top."

Suddenly the mynah came swooping in.

"Now where did you come from? Have you finished the grains 1 had kept for you last evening?"

Salu and the others looked puzzled at his talk. Then, Minguel stopped abruptly, feeling sheepish.

Coiling the rope and hoisting it on his shoulders, Rocky climbed up the tree. He had almost reached the top, when Salu called out, "That's enough. Why are you climbing higher?"

"Quiet!" Rocky climbed higher. "A mynah has built a nest at the top. There seem to be some fledglings."

Fledglings? My salori has hatched little mynahs! And this Rocky is climbing to the top to get them!

"You there, Rocky! Get down first," Minguel's voice rose. "You get down from that tree!" He was almost shouting.

The labourer stopped midway. "Don't shout Bhatkar. They'll fly off. Keep them for you if you want."

"No, no. First you get down. Get down, I say!" Minguel was almost spluttering.

Rocky started climbing down. Salu was surprised and

confused. Patting Minguel on the shoulder, he reasoned, "Listen, Mingloo. When we cut the tree, the nest will fall and the little birds will die. Instead of that, let them take out the nest."

It was as if someone had struck Minguel on the head. He stared around, stunned. The labourer had scrambled down the tree, and this brought Minguel to a more even keel.

"No, no!" he said hoarsely. "Don't cut the tree! Those little birds, they are my mynah's ..."

Salu did not know whether to laugh or cry. "What's wrong with you, Mingloo?"

"Salu, cut it later if you want, but not so soon. Those little ones must learn to fly. Take the tree after that. In a few days time –" Minguel pleaded.

"Who wants it later? Yesterday you made a deal and today you back out of it?" Salu asked crossly.

"Salu, please do me a favour. Spare this tree. I will return your money."

Salu was taken aback. He paused for a moment, and then asked loudly, "And who will pay these men for their effort and time? You have to - and now I'll have to go to Remedios. You have needlessly wasted two days of mine!"

Reassured that Salu had agreed, Minguel turned to the labourers. "My dear boys, I'm a poor man. I have been the cause of wasting your time – I'll give you something for tea. Please forgive me." Minguel pleaded with folded hands.

The men could only look at each other with surprise.

Minguel started going down on his knees, when Rocky stopped him.

"Look here Bhatkar, we are not greedy. But we have lost half a day. Pay us half-day's wages."

Persuading the labourers to accept twenty five rupees each instead of half of their customary eighty rupees, Minguel hurried inside. Feliza had guessed what was happening. Ignoring her questioning glance, Minguel went to the money box, pulled out a few notes, and handed over the fifty rupees advanced by Salu back to him, and parted with another fifty for the labourers. He came in, having watched them go away. "You know Feliza, my mynah has hatched some little ones," he said. "She's made a nest in a hollow right at the top of our dead coconut tree."

He waited for a tirade from a furious Feliza at the squandering of a hundred rupees.

Instead, here she was, bubbling with excitement, "And you know Mingloo, the little squirrel ate that whole mango slice. I'll cut another mango. Tonight, we'll keep two slices."

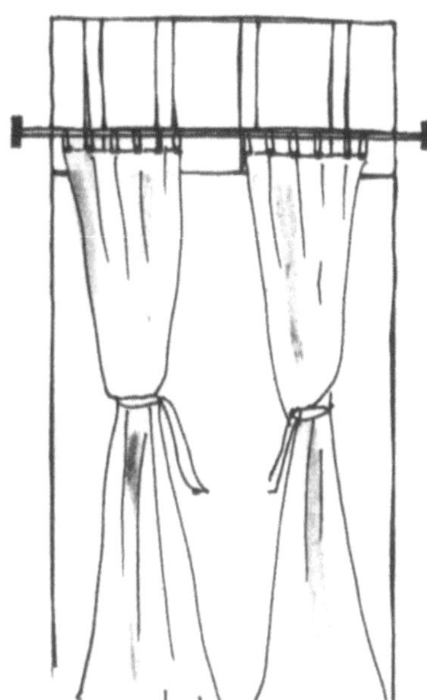

The Red Nissan

Kuwaitkar. The very word conjures up a certain image of the Goan in Kuwait before our eyes. This family did not conform to that stereotype.

There are two classes of Goans living in Kuwait. The group of unskilled and semi-skilled workers who come without their spouses and live in cramped quarters, with four and more sharing a room, who toil for ten to twelve hours a day and scrape together some meagre savings. The other class is that of the literate white-collared people who work in offices. These generally come in with their families. The wives often work as secretaries, at times earning more than their husbands. They stay in comfortable rented apartments, sometimes shared by two families, with all sorts of modern amenities and gadgets. After an eight-hour shift at the office, they are free to drive down to the supermarket to shop and socialize.

But there was yet another breed – one that wallowed in supreme luxury. I discovered this when I went to Maria's house.

Since my tour to Kuwait was an official one, the arrangements for my stay had been made by the Indian Embassy. The day after I landed, I phoned Maria to tell her that I was in Kuwait. "Keep Friday free for us," Maria said. "Don't accept any other engagement for that day."

I knew that Maria was quite well-off. I had heard that Maria's husband had built a bungalow in the upmarket locality of Altinho in Panjim. Other Kuwaitkars too, who spoke of her, contributed to my impression that Maria was doing very well for herself. But I had never imagined that my estimate would be so badly off-target.

Arthur himself came to the hotel to escort me home. I had seen the Governor's Cadillac in Goa, but this one made my eyes pop. It was sleek and shiny, a posh jet-black beauty on the outside. And the interiors were even more opulent.

The car itself gave me a fair idea of his affluence. But I couldn't be too sure. He might have borrowed it from

somebody, or it may have been the company's car! As I mulled this over in my mind, we arrived at his bungalow.

All the bungalows at Mushrif are luxurious. There are no apartments or flats here, only elegant villas amid spacious grounds, neat gardens or tennis lawns.

Arthur opened the door with his key. "Hi! How nice to see you here!" Maria welcomed me in English. She looked quite different in a salwar kameez.

"You look good, Maria," I complimented her. "This outfit suits you."

"Oh, come on. These are my house rags!"

I didn't know what to make of this. Was she putting it on or was she bragging that her wardrobe was far more elaborate?

I was about to sit on the sofa in the living room, but Maria stopped me. "Not there, that's for formal guests! Come inside."

The inner room was a pleasant arrangement for about eight or ten intimate friends. I was truly impressed by all the magnificence I saw.

My friendship with Maria went back to our childhood. Her father was a doctor so the family was well-known throughout the village. He was our family doctor too. And since we were neighbours, we ended up becoming good friends. Later, our family left the village and settled down in Panjim. Our comradeship ought to have ended then. But Maria was married in Panjim and since we used to run into each other from time to time, our friendship remained alive. Maria's husband was in Kuwait, and came down to Goa every year. I knew him only from a few occasional meetings. Later, Maria too joined her husband in Kuwait. We hadn't seen each other for quite some time. After a gap of some years, I met her when she had come down last August. She said she was in a hurry, but had talked for a long time. She spoke of how her husband's hectic business schedule left little time for anything else and how taxing her children's school curriculum was. She fretted about the children who were presently holidaying in England. Before taking her leave, I hinted that I might visit Kuwait on some official work. She fished out a card from her purse at once and said, "Phone me the moment you land in Kuwait, and do come and stay with us."

Because of the warmth of Maria's invitation, I had phoned her and had thus landed at their place.

"Where are the children? At school?" I asked.

"Today's a holiday isn't it?" Maria reminded me that it was Friday. "Hold on! I'll introduce you to them." She rang the bell.

The maid appeared. She looked like a Goan, but Maria spoke to her in English. "Please call both the girls here."

I didn't recall having met Maria's children before. "I thought you had three children, Maria," I said.

"Yes, but our little boy is in England. At a public school," Arthur said.

I felt a twinge of pity for the poor child. "How does he like it?"

"Let's see!" Arthur sighed. "We've admitted him just this year."

"He'll like it fine. It's only his Dad who can't do without

him!" There was more asperity than fondness in Maria's tone, I felt.

Just then, the girls came skipping down the stairs. Maria introduced us. "This is Sharon, the elder one, and this one is Milan. Indian name! How does it sound?" I laughed. Apart from the name, nothing else was Indian. The hair was cropped short, while the clothes and accent were all foreign.

Sharon must have been around sixteen or seventeen, but she looked like a mature young woman in her twenties. She had a full figure, and bold, worldly-wise eyes that spoke of many an adventurous tryst. The second one, Milan, was twelve or thirteen, with a pleasant face and innocent flitting eyes. Both had worn flimsy tops. Sharon wore jeans, while Milan was in a mini skirt.

I had heard that in Kuwait, one had to cover the body completely, and must admit that I was surprised at these precious specimens.

After tea, Sharon said, "Mom, we're going skating."

"Come back soon," Maria said, in English. "You know that we're going to Al Zor, don't you?"

"In that case, I'll go to the club with them, otherwise they may not come back soon," Arthur said, getting up.

"You're always like this," Maria said crossly. "Let them go alone. As if you have to chaperone them!"

Arthur didn't reply. He got up, excused himself and went out with his daughters.

"They never miss their ice-skating on Fridays," Maria explained.

I was amazed. "Ice-skating in Kuwait? And in this hot weather?" I asked.

Maria burst out laughing. "It doesn't snow here, but there's a special ice-skating rink at the club."

Maria then spoke enthusiastically about her children. "The British Ambassador lives in the next bungalow - his daughter is a close friend of Sharon's. Sharon's even gone to England with her." I heard accounts of how much they spent on their children's education. They were students of the New English School, run by the British Embassy. Sharon had finished, but Milan was still in school. Each one's education came to nothing less than twenty five thousand Kuwaiti dinars. Besides that, every year, they were taken for a camp to England and so on.

I ventured gently about the restrictions there. "Tell me Maria, is it permitted here to wear the clothes your girls are dressed in? I had heard that it was obligatory to cover yourself."

Once again Maria burst out laughing. "All that depends on the society you move in!"

"And maintaining this standard of living must cost a bomb! That car alone –"

Maria cut me short. "You have only seen one of them. We have three. Our Sharon is a speed freak - she loves fast cars. Just the other day she bought a new car, the latest sports model from Nissan! Arthur gets the shivers when Sharon drives."

I asked one last question. "Maria, forgive me if I'm being curious, but how can you afford all this?"

"My dear fellow, if you manage to succeed in business in Kuwait, you can" just rake in the bucks. Arthur has a big business in construction materials. Even after paying off his Arab partner, we can afford to live like this. And if this Iran-Iraq war were not going on, we would have covered our house in Goa with tiles of gold!"

While we were still talking, Arthur came in with the girls, who promptly went to sleep exhausted.

They had planned to be at Al Zor beach by noon. The food, soft drinks, water and a flask full of tea was packed and ready. But though it was past noon, we had still not left for the beach. Maria was bustling about. It was obvious that the girls didn't want to come with us, but she finally managed to coax them into coming along. As we were leaving the house, Sharon imposed her condition, 'T'll come in my car; you go in yours."

Arthur objected, but Maria intervened saying she would handle it – "Okay. We'll go ahead and you follow right behind."

Finally, we set out to the beach, with Maria, Arthur and I in the black Cadillac and Sharon with Milan in the red Sports car.

It is a hundred and five kilo metres from Kuwait to Al Zor beach – an hour's drive. Barely five minutes after we had started, Sharon's car whizzed past us and left us far behind. Arthur fumed, but Maria remained calm.

At the Fahil-Ahmadi junction, the police were checking vehicles. I hadn't realized it till then, but I had left the pouch with my passport at Maria's place. Arthur grew nervous for a moment when he heard this, but quickly composed himself. "Don't worry. Let's see what happens." The car inched forward. The policeman examined Arthur's akamo, the identity card to be compulsorily carried by aliens in Kuwait at all times. He then looked at Maria, and signalled us to move on.

"The prestige of a Cadillac," explained Maria. "Otherwise, they check each person thoroughly."

"Now where have these two got to?" Arthur looked around frantically. Momentarily distracted, he hesitated at the highway. The police officer ahead, waved us to a stop. Once again, Arthur was asked for his identification. He then stared in my direction and thrust forward his hand for mine.

I broke out in a cold sweat. I had heard that the first thing they do, without caring who you might be, is to dump you into jail.

Arthur tried to explain to the police officer in Arabic, but the man wouldn't budge an inch. Ordering the car to be parked, he turned his attention to other vehicles.

Ten tense minutes crawled by.

Arthur worried about the girls who had gone ahead.

Maria was anxious that the girls would have to wait for us at the beach while we were stuck here.

And, looming large before me, was the Kuwait lockup!

Arthur got out of the car and once again tried to reason out with the police officer, "If you won't believe me, let him remain here. I will go back, bring his passport and return in twenty minutes."

The officer was unmoved by Arthur's plea.

Arthur tried another tack. "A short while ago, my daughters went ahead in a red Nissan. Please let us go or else we will miss them." Immediately the Arab policeman gave a low whistle, mumbled something in Arabic under his breath, and clicking his fingers, he motioned for us to go. Heaving a sigh of relief, we started off towards Al Zor.

Sharon's red car was nowhere in sight.

"I told you that we should go in one car," Arthur was grumbling.

"Never mind. They aren't babies, are they?" responded Maria tersely.

"Didn't she say that she'd follow us? Where are they now?" Arthur was at boiling point.

"Don't go on and on Arthur! She isn't new to this road. She'll be there. She may even be waiting for us on the way." Maria sounded exasperated.

We drove on in silence. Arthur was doing a hundred to a hundred and twenty kmph, but there were cars that still zoomed past us. Further to our left were the oncoming lanes. On the way, we could see several smashed-up vehicles involved in accidents, but residents of Kuwait didn't give them a second glance. On the highway, practically every kilometre had a burnt-out car shell or an overturned vehicle.

About half an hour later, we saw a red Nissan. An overturned one.

I started in spite of myself, and looked at Maria. She appeared nervous. Arthur had already eased back on the pedal.

We came abreast the car, and Arthur jammed his foot

back on the accelerator. For no apparent reason he laughed. "They must have reached long back," he remarked.

"Our Sharon doesn't need more than forty five minutes to reach Al Zor from Kuwait," Maria added with a short laugh. I breathed a sigh of relief.

Soon, we were at Al Zor.

Al Zor is a popular beach. Countless cars were parked by the roadside. We scanned the line of cars for about one and a half kilo metres. Sharon's car was nowhere to be seen. We reversed the entire length as well, looking out anxiously, but there was no sign of the red Nissan.

"We drove very fast because we assumed they might be here," said Maria. "I wonder if they were looking for us, waiting somewhere around that junction."

"In that case, we'll hang around here for a while," suggested Arthur.

So we sat in the car, looking at all the vehicles coming in from Kuwait. But there wasn't a single red car among them. We waited and waited.

"Could they be at the Family Beach further down?" wondered Arthur.

Maria looked visibly nervous by now. "Let's check."

"But what if they come here while we are there? If you could both wait here for a short while, I'll dash there for a look and come back," decided Arthur.

We waited. "Don't worry," I tried to comfort Maria. "They'll be okay."

"You can't be sure of that in Kuwait!" Maria blurted out. "These Arabs in Kuwait are dangerous! Do you know what

that Arab cop said to Arthur when he whistled? He said, So those coquettes are your daughters! That's why Arthur was upset."

Arthur returned. "They're not there either. What do we do?"

"Let's go back. They must be home," I said. By now, we had completely forgotten that we had come to enjoy ourselves on the beach.

"Sometimes these Arabs can he quite rowdy." Arthur said as if to himself. "I have always been saying that those clothes aren't suitable for girls, not here in Kuwait at least!"

Maria was silent. Between the woman who had come to the beach and the one who was now returning, there was a gulf as wide as that between Europe and India.

Glancing at the many accident-wrecked cars strewn on the roadside and doing our best to push away our worries, we returned to Kuwait.

We reached Mushrif. And right there at the doorway, stood the red Nissan sports car.

Maria laughed. "I knew it all along!"

As Evening Fades

It was pitch dark outside when Mangalakka's eyes opened. It had been like this of late. A veil of sleep would stretch over her eyes at dusk, and flit away well before dawn. At first, Mangalakka struggled to sleep, but once disturbed, it simply drifted away. In any case, it wasn't as though there were any chores to attend to once she woke up. What was to be done, then? As a compromise, Mangalakka had perfected the middle path of lazing in bed, waiting for dawn.

But the interval between her wakefulness and daybreak was so long that her mind usually lifted off, gently spread its wings and soared into the sky of memory. Admittedly, hers was a limited horizon. She was fifty four years old. A couple of tempests had buffeted her life, and most of the leaves of memory had blown away into oblivion. But there were a few precious memories that she had hoarded in the recesses of her mind.

She had been married the year before Goa's Liberation from Portuguese rule. At that time, her name had been Kalavati, the name given to her by her parents. Everyone had liked it. She had herself felt that she liked her name more than the reflection that stared back at her in the mirror. She had studied up to middle school, but had to go to Karwar to take the exam, and Karwar those days was foreign soil. You needed a passport and visa to get there those days. So her father had not sent her.

Her father's business was thriving. The year before her marriage, he had bought a car, an Opel Rekord. The whole family including Kalavati was thrilled! That was about the time that some matchmaker had taken her proposal to Shiri. This young man from Loliem was supposed to come to see the girl. His people, it seemed, wanted a bride from town.

All decked up in finery, Kalavati had entered the living room with a tray of tea. Suddenly, her eyes fell on a kitten standing at the window. She had always had a morbid fear of dogs and cats. The tray in her hand began to wobble. Her brother Prakash had nudged her forward.

"Whom are you scared of? Nobody's going to eat you!"

They began to tease her after Shiri left. She insisted that she had been neither shy nor scared of Shiri, and that it was the cat at the window that had made her nervous. Nobody believed her then. Later, though, they found that the stray kitten kept returning even after being shooed away. After two days of unsuccessful chasing, Prakash stuffed it into a bag. He took Kalavati along in the Opel to convince her of the kitten's absence, and left the small animal far from the house. Returning home, they found the matchmaker inside, smiling brightly.

"They have approved of the girl!" he announced triumphantly. And turning to Kalavati, "Now make me some tea with your own hands."

What would it be like to live in a rustic Loliem, so faraway!

"Aiyee, please," Kalavati pleaded with her mother. "How will I manage in such a distant godforsaken place?" But her protests had no effect. Everybody was thrilled that the girl had got through the test in the very first attempt. In the end, Kalavati had to accept defeat.

Shiri had promptly exercised the prerogative of a Hindu husband to name his bride as he chose. "From now on, we'll call you Mangala. How do you like it?" Kalavati had been silent. Then, she had nodded slightly in acquiescence. From then on, she became Shiri's Mangala. In course of time the honorific of "akka" or elder sister attached itself to her name.

Once married, there was no question of any regret. Shiri

had heaped her with love. By the time she had settled down in her new house and learnt the ropes of village life, Shiri's elderly mother died. Mangala was expecting Prabhakar at the time, and had gone to her parental house in Margao for her confinement.

One day, an agitated Shiri had turned up in Margao unexpectedly. He came with the news that the Indian troops had massed on the border and that the Portuguese garrison at the Polem outpost was fleeing in disarray. Shiri was excited, but Mangala's father and brother had grown pensive. They were quick to express their misgivings. There would be war and this would take its toll on business. Goa may well be burnt to cinders!

Shiri had set out to go back to Loliem immediately, but Mangala had fervently pleaded with him not to, in view of the perilous situation. That very day, her labour pains began. She bore it for two days. The Indian army was entering Goa. Rumours were rife that the retreating Portuguese had blown up bridges and that the Indian troops had seized control of the airport, but she could barely get the picture between contractions. And Prabhakar was born exactly on the day of Goa's Liberation.

"Once, there was a king, and a queen and a prince," went Mangala's own fairy tale that she regaled Prabhakar with. And then, with Shiri's sudden death just before his fortieth birthday, the fairy tale had turned into a nightmare.

Right from the beginning, she hadn't liked the idea of Shiri buying a motorcycle. She had never forgotten the pleasure of her father's car and had been prodding Shiri to buy one too, but Shiri had gone in for a motorcycle even without asking her. Left with no alternative, Mangalakka reconciled herself to the motorbike. In fact, on that fateful day, Mangala was supposed to have gone with Shiri, but because the government offices in Canacona would be closed by the time she finished her household chores, Shiri had gone alone.

And he was gone for eternity.

The truck struck him from behind, and Shiri had gone right under its wheels. They brought the body covered. She didn't even get to see his face. Living seemed futile, she thought, caught in the depths of grief and anguish. But innocent Prabha had clung to her neck, pacifying her.

I will make my Prabha an engineer, Shiri would say. Mangalakka resolved to fulfil his dreams, and clamped down on her sorrow.

Mangalakka had never quite enjoyed real happiness. But it was her nature to find her equilibrium no matter what situation she was in, and so she didn't buckle under even in moments of overwhelming catastrophe. Now, she took all of Shiri's responsibilities upon herself and especially took care not to neglect Prabhakar's studies.

Just as the social upheaval set in motion by the 'land to the landless' legislation called the Mundkar Act began, she called her tenants and settled a via media with them that both satisfied their aspirations and didn't pull her down into a mire of costly litigation. Even in difficult times, she didn't run to her brother for help. Fully aware of what she was doing, she freely signed away her

rights in her brother's favour when, after their parents' death, he came to her for a waiver to her parental estate, thus keeping him indebted to her. When Prabhakar started straying into the family business of coconut and betelnut cultivation much to the detriment of his studies, Mangalakka steeled herself and approached her brother, upon which he gladly took upon himself the responsibility of educating Prabhakar up to high school. Staying in the college hostel, Prabhakar finished his pre-university studies with a high percentage, and managed to get admission into the prestigious Indian Institute of Technology at Powai in Bombay.

These and the good job he had secured soon after getting his engineering degree were instances that evoked mixed feelings in Mangalakka. Were she and Prabha to be separated for all time? Would this become a permanent arrangement? But then, wasn't it all her own doing?

But years of forbearance yielded fruit. His company was setting up a plant in Goa, and Prabha was transferred to Goa as the Chief Chemical Engineer. He took his mother to live with him in his bungalow in Panjim. Staying with her son in his bungalow gave Mangalakka immense happiness.

Then came Prabhakar's marriage to Namita. And with it, the redundancy of a mother in the world of her son and daughter-in-law, and now her repatriation to Loliem.

Shifting the forearm that was covering her eyes, Mangalakka strained to see if she could catch the distant rays of daybreak. It was pitch black outside. Turning to her side, she closed her eyes again. Today was Saturday, but Prabha wouldn't be coming. He had written in his letter: "The doctor has advised Namita complete bed rest, so I won't be able to come for the next two months."

The letter was a month old, which meant that Prabha wouldn't be visiting her for another month. Another month of complete loneliness. She sighed, surprised at herself. "Why am I distressed?"she wondered. "Because Prabha won't be coming? Because I shall be all alone? Because he doesn't care about me? Sh-i-i! Why am I being so selfish? I should have been worried about Namita! The doctor's advised her complete rest. Prabha must be reeling under all that strain! He must be managing Namita's chores too. In fact, Prabhakar should have told me. He should have called me. I didn't leave after a furious quarrel, did I? I may not get along famously with Namita but then, which mother and daughter-in-law have ever hit it off? But, in this hour of their need, shouldn't she – shouldn't both of them have remembered me? All they had to do was ask, Aiyee, could you come to us? Had I ever stood on prestige?"

Prabha had always been away from her. First, he had gone to school and pre-university in Margao and later in Bombay. Her house became a home only during the holidays. When he studied for his engineering degree, he would come home just once a year. As soon as his results were announced, he had received an offer from the well-known Watson Chemicals Limited. It had been a period of conflicting emotions for her. She was genuinely proud of

Prabha's achievements but the distance that stretched away between them saddened her. Mangalakka pulled through the days consoling herself with the thought that someday, the separation would end.

And so it happened that Prabha was transferred to Goa. The memory of the day he came to take Mangalakka to stay with him in his company's bungalow was still etched deeply in her mind.

The transition from the comforts of urban life in Margao to the rustic village life of Loliem had left Mangala traumatized. She had used Shiri's mother's death as an excuse to try and persuade her husband to move. "Let's build a house in Margao or Panjim," she had cajoled. "I feel lost in this village house." But Shiri had parried away the suggestion every time. With time, Mangala had stopped asking. But when she went to live with Prabha, Mangala's shrunken veins began to pulsate with life.

The bungalow and everything in it had been planned beautifully. Mangala had fallen in love with the neat, modern kitchen. Prabha himself showed her how to operate the gas range, mixer and other gadgets. Within a week, she had mastered them all. And, one day when she was in a good mood, Prabha had confided his secret to her.

"Aiyee, I'd like to share some good news with you." And thrusting a photograph into Mangalakka's hand, he said, "This is Namita. She's from Mumbai. I want to bring her into this house as your daughter-in-law."

Mangalakka still couldn't fathom why she had reacted

the way she had, that moment. She ought to have gushed, "What a smart boy you have been! You know how anxious I have been to see the face of my daughter-in-law, but you never even gave me an inkling! And she's so pretty! Really, you both are made for each other. Like a perfect, divine Lakshmi-Narayan couple! Now tell me, when are you bringing her to meet me?"

Instead, so many questions crowded her mind: How long has he known her? So this was why he would go dumb whenever the subject of proposals and marriage came up! Why did he have to hide it all from me? How many people I had approached to find a nice girl for him! Couldn't he have told me right in the beginning? Is he telling me now, after he's already made up his mind?

She should have congratulated him, but she stayed silent. Did her eyes register the receding spectacle of marriage proposals coming to her doorstep from deferential parents of prospective brides? Or was her maternal ego hurt?

"Aiyee, why are you so quiet?"

"Prabha, you have told me all this after deciding everything yourself. If you had asked me – Aiyee, may I marry this girl? – do you think I would have objected?"

I should never have said that to him, she thought. He came to me with such enthusiasm, I shouldn't have spiked his happiness like that.

Later, Mangalakka consoled herself and started working wholeheartedly. The wedding was in Bombay. It was a grand celebration. But she wasn't sure if she could call it a

marriage. There was neither the kanyadan – the sacred ritual of offering the daughter in marriage – nor a priestly bhat to bless it. They didn't even bother about the muhurat, the auspicious timing! Good that Prabha had told her about all this in advance. She was at least mentally prepared. Neither Prabha nor Namita were religious, so they had chosen to get married this way, with a ceremony at the registrar's and a lavish reception thereafter. She knew that Prabha hadn't accepted any dowry. Rather, she had approved of it. But a wedding without a religious ceremony?

"Prabha, you must at least do the saptapati!" Mangala had insisted on the seven steps around the holy fire.

"Aiyee, you had these meaningless rituals at your marriage, didn't you? Why did you become a widow at such a young age, then? Let us have it our own way."

The harsh logic left her with no answers. Silently, she swallowed it all. Prabha's in-laws were well off, and had spent lavishly on the decorations and wedding feasts. Mangalakka said to Prabha the next day, "Better tell Namita's father that we'll pay half the expenses."

Prabha began to laugh. "Aiyee, they're filthy rich. Besides, Daddy would be hurt if I asked."

Though they were very rich, they appeared to be simple and affectionate. In the beginning, the big-city atmosphere of Bombay almost seemed to suffocate Mangalakka, but Narnita's parents made her feel so comfortable that she no longer felt like a stranger. Namita too fussed over Mangalakka, solicitously calling her Aiyee.

But the inherent differences didn't take long to crop

up. When she had closed the house in Loliem and come to stay in the bungalow in Panjim, Mangalakka had taken down the idols from the devaro, the family altar, wrapped them in the muktto, the sacred silken cloth, and brought them with her. She had then reserved a corner for them in the bungalow. At that time, she had not noticed Prabha's forehead creasing in disapproval. But ever since Namita's arrival, Mangalakka was puzzled to see the frown on her forehead every day.

She didn't know what she had done to cause offence. But she was very careful to avoid any friction. When the first cutting that she had planted in front of the bungalow sprouted a beautiful rose, Mangalakka's first thought was to offer it to god. But before that Namita simply snipped it away and tucked it into her hair. Mangalakka had been silent. But one day, when Namita was walking towards where Magalakka prayed, nonchalantly clicking her high-heeled sandals, a pained Mangalakka could contain herself no longer. "Please remove your sandals when you're near the deity!" she burst out. Namita said nothing, but stormed out of the room. The next day, Prabha came to his mother, and told her to move the idols to her bedroom.

He, of course, gave his mother her due respect. Namita too was never disrespectful. Mangalakka knew that she too, in her own way, was trying to understand her motherlaw. She was aware that a certain amount of friction was inevitable. Which was why Mangalakka continued to take things in her stride. There was also some degree of self-interest that her son should not be alienated from her.

Mangalakka had always wanted Shiri to buy a car. That wish had remained unfulfilled during his lifetime. When Prabha bought a car soon after the wedding, no one could have been happier. Prabha too, was aware of his mother's unfulfilled desire. He had taken his mother and wife for a ride to Loliem. Whenever they went to the beach at Miramar or Dona Paula, he would take his mother along.

It didn't take Mangalakka long to sense that Namita didn't like this. Thereafter, whenever Prabha asked her to accompany them on a ride, Mangalakka would wave him away saying, "You two carry on." It was only when the two of them left that she felt utterly desolate. There were some houses close by, and Mangalakka thought it would help while away the time if she could befriend some of the neighbours and have a chat, now and then. Her plans were thwarted unexpectedly by Namita, who said, very firmly, "I don't approve of your going there or anybody coming here!"

Prabha, in whose presence all this had happened, reasoned, "Aiyee, there's a big difference between people from the village and people from the city. Over here, everyone tends to take advantage of your simplicity. Namita's a Bombay girl, she's speaking from experience."

Mangalakka, who had had to endure compromises all her life but had never sacrificed her self-respect so far, slowly began to feel uneasy. She was filled with pride when me thought of Prabha's bungalow, Prabha's car, and Prabha's phone, but the restrictions that wound themselves around her life choked her.

One day, there was a party at Prabha's house. A wet party, apparently! "My friends are coming," Prabha had told her. "Try and stay in your room." He had brought in a chef who cooked a variety of special dishes for the party. Soon, Prabha's friends began to troop in with their wives. The house began to reek of alcohol. Even the women were sipping beer! Mangalakka couldn't contain herself.

"I'm going to be frank, Aiyee," Prabha said the next day, when she questioned him in front of her daughter-in-law, about the previous day's doings. "I have hesitated about having a party here all these days because of your presence. These events are held every now and then at one another's houses. We can't avoid hosting them. When we live in society, and we're connected to business, we have to entertain. You must try to understand. We have to move with the times, right?"

In that case, you should have put a glass in my hand too! – the words were on the tip of her tongue. But she swallowed the thought and went inside.

Changing times had probably made it necessaty to have such parties. It was quite possible. It isn't as if Prabha drinks a lot, but until yesterday, I didn't even know that Prabha even took alcohol!

She became restless. Worry tormented her. Worry of what? Of the times that were changing? Or of Prabha, who had changed?

It wasn't as if Mangalakka was the kind of woman who blindly followed rituals. She was certainly religious, and followed a few traditions. After a bath, she offered

incense and flowers to the deity and that was that. Her only concern was that the puja room and the kitchen ought to be undefiled. But ever since she had come to Prabha's house, her uneasiness had only begun to increase.

Chanda, the maid who came every morning, washed the clothes and utensils, swept the floor, cleaned the fish and sometimes did the cooking as well. She usually left in the afternoon, after lunch. She didn't come as usual, one day, and Mangalakka took the cooking and sweeping upon herself. Despite her daughter-in-law's protests, she even washed the utensils. Late in the evening, Chanda came, gave Namita a pan of bityani, and left.

That night, Prabha and Namita ate the biryani with great relish. It must have been good; its aroma made Mangalakka's mouth water. She didn't eat it, however, as she was observing her Thursday fast. "Your biryani was good, it seems," she remarked to Chanda the next day. "How did you make it?"

Chanda gave her the recipe. "We sprinkle meat fat on the top," she added. "That's what gives it that delicious taste."

A sneaking suspicion took root within Mangalakka. She asked casually, "What was the occasion at your home yesterday?"

"Don't you know that yesterday was our Id?"

Shocked, Mangalakka rushed to Namita at once. "Do you know who Chanda is?"

"What do you mean, who she is?"

"She's a Muslim!"

Namita looked as calm as ever. "What of it?"

It was enough to make Mangalakka lose her composure. They had a heated argument and the tirade went on, even after Prabha came home in the evening.

"Do what you want. Keep away from god, forget about religion, but why drag me down to hell with you? All these days I have eaten what she's cooked, and neither of you even bothered to tell me that she was a Muslim, and to make it worse, both of you even ate the meat she cooked!"

In a patient voice, Prabha said, "She may be a Muslim or Christian – as long as she's clean, that's all that matters. The old days of caste and religious differences are over now."

Namita didn't interfere. But now, there was unanimity on at least one point as a result of the spat between mother and son. What was done, was done. The past was at an end. Henceforth, all the household chores came under the purview of Chanda – everything except the cooking. That was to be the exclusive domain of Mangalakka; out of bounds for the maid.

One day, Mangalakka came down with fever. She thought Namita would cook but it was Chanda who entered the kitchen. Mangalakka didn't touch a morsel during her two days of fever. With the realization that with the changing times, she too had to change, she finally accepted defeat.

When there was no "good news" in the offing after more than a year of their marriage, Mangalakka tried to broach the subject of children with them. When she gathered her courage and suggested that her daughter-in-law undertake either Sankashti or Vinayaki, the ritual fasts

on the fourth and nineteenth days of the Hindu month recommended for the fulfilment of wishes, Prabha and Namita burst out laughing.

She never brought up the subject again.

There was a festival of religious songs at the Cultural Centre that Mangalakka was keen on attending. She was sure that Prabha wouldn't object. But she decided not to go, for fear of them both ridiculing her.

But how could she keep mum even after witnessing Chanda's brazen act? That day, she had brought the roof down.

Chanda was about to leave for home after lunch. Mangalakka was at the door, waiting to shut it. As Chanda swept past, her bag thudded against the door in a way that roused Mangalakka's suspicion. Swiftly, she thrust het hand into the bag and pulled out half of the coconut they had cracked open just that morning. Trained as she had been from childhood to believe that a household with such leakages wouldn't take long to be emptied, Mangalakka's annoyance reached new levels. She would expose her now, this very instant. "You thief!" she cried out, beginning her interrogation. The loud voice attracted Namita's attention, who walked up and without even asking what the matter was, retorted with a "Don't shout like this!"

Mangalakka was stunned. A feeling of faintness assailed her, an opportunity that Chanda was quick to utilize. "Memsaab, I was just taking this half-coconut," she said in an apologetic tone. "I wanted to tell you, but I forgot.

I'm so sorry, but I am not a thief!" Namita let her leave, and also told her to take the half-coconut.

Mangalakka didn't break her vow of silence till Prabha came home in the evening, whereupon Namita gave Prabha her version of the incident.

It wasn't long before Prabha came to his mother. "Aiyee, there's no doubt that Chanda was stealing," he said in his usual, suave tone. "But it's just a half-coconut. You can't brand her a thief for taking something worth just a couple of rupees. Where are we going to get another trained maid if we sack Chanda? She serves us well. Don't talk to her about anything in future, will you, Aiyee? Do keep an eye on things, but ignore the minor problems. If you notice anything, just tell Namita or me. We'll all be in trouble if Chanda stops working."

She could neither understand nor digest this. All night long, she tossed and turned, unable to sleep. The house in Loliem was better for her, she realized, than this bungalow here in Panjim. That house is mine. This is Prabha's and Namita's. Chanda is much more valuable to them than I! How long will I go on, caught in the middle?

Her mind was made up. Tomorrow? Yes, tomorrow!

But the next day, Chanda didn't report for work in the morning. Namita was upset; Prabha was worried too. Mangalakka was amazed at the distress they were both in, faced with the task of running the bungalow without Chanda. She had managed the house in Loliem single-handedly all these years, and no one had ever commended her for it! And it hadn't been just a house

either; she had run the entire household and family. She had even supervised the work in the coconut, betel and cashew plantations. Shouldn't Prabha have at least realized this? But then, how would he? She had taken such pains to shelter him from all that. While it was true that she had begun to feel her age, of late, Mangalakka was quite prepared to shoulder the task of running the bungalow if Chanda didn't turn up. The thought was actually quite uplifting.

"Let her not come if she doesn't. It's not a difficult job – I'll take care of everything."

But Prabha was annoyed. "Aiyee, running a bungalow's no joke. Washing the clothes, scrubbing vessels, mopping the floor, watering the garden – can you handle all that?"

She could have said yes. But Prabha's question carried a built-in negative connotation – that she couldn't do it!

Shiri's mother had passed away when she was expecting. Before her death, Mangalakka had nursed her through her illness, and at the same time kept the house going. After her mother-in-law's death and until the last day of her pregnancy, Mangalakka had done all the household chores, alone. Shiri had been so proud of her!

Namita and Prabha went out together, the next day. Apparently, they went to Chanda's home, saying, "What's happened has happened. We have let it all go. You must forget it too, and come back." They may not have stopped with that equivocation. God knows if they even apologized to her! They came back, looking rather pleased. Chanda had apparently agreed to resume from the next day.

Prabha left for office, having dropped Namita home. Mangalakka didn't get a chance to speak to him and so she stayed on in Panjim. That afternoon, there was a phone call from Mumbai. As Prabha entered the house, Namita gave him the glad tidings, "Daddy's arriving in Goa tomorrow by the first flight." Prabha too appeared buoyed up with the news. Mangalakka couldn't share in their happiness; she was much too fatigued, mentally and physically. She managed to speak to Prabha before her son and daughter-in-law went for their evening walk. "I think I'll go and stay in Loliem for a few days. An occasional eye has to be kept on the things there. Put me on the first bus tomorrow. I should be there by noon."

That was her last night in Panjim. Son and daughter-in-law had been silent when she broached her plans to leave, as if they found her proposal agreeable. She rose early the next morning, and packed her things. Namita stood by, as she wrapped her idols in the silk mukutt. It would have made her feel better if the girl had asked, "Aiyee, why take the idols if you're going for just a few days?" Or was she quiet because she felt a little guilty?

As she was leaving Namita said, "Take care, Aiyee." When Prabha opened his purse and took out some money, Mangalakka refused in such a firm tone that he was momentarily taken aback. He put the money back and picked up his briefcase, explaining that he couldn't escort her to Loliem since he had to go to office. On the other hand, he did know that he had to go to the airport to pick up his father-in-law. When she left,

Mangalakka saw that they both had synthetic smiles pasted on their faces.

Prabha left after seating her in the bus. A three-hour journey later, Mangalakka reached Loliem.

The next Sunday, Prabha came to Loliem with Namita and Daddy. The orchards, bubbling brooks, the rambling house built around the open square razangann and the clean environs – all came in for lavish praise from Daddy. Prabha had brought some fish, and Mangalakka set to work immediately, and by one thirty in the afternoon, she had finished cooking Prabha's favourite khatkhatem, a vegetable potpourri. Everybody relished it. Prabha and Namita behaved as if nothing had happened. When they went back in the evening, Mangalakka reasoned that nothing had actually happened between them that could be construed as wrong. Could I have done something wrong, she wondered. Or am I imagining things? But then, shouldn't they have said, Aiyee, you said you would stay in Loliem for just a few days. Come now, let's go back. Or at least, When are you coming to us, Aiyee?

She heaved a huge sigh that seemed to expel all the air from her whole body, and turned over. The cat sleeping on the quilt at her feet, awoke, disturbed, and turned round and round, seeking a more comfortable position. Then it went back to sleep. Up in the heaven, Shiri must be amazed that Mangalakka had a cat for a pet – one with which she shared her own bed too!

She smiled, eyelids heavy with sleep. Cats. She had hated them more than any other animal species, right from her childhood. Shiri's house had a huge tomcat, and she had been scared out of her wits the first time it came near her! And that was it. It became a standing joke in the household that the new bride was terrified of the cat. That animal too, had seemed to love brushing himself against her at every opportunity. But she wouldn't let him, and as soon as she had settled herself in her husband's affections, she had insisted that he give away the cat. Shiri, however, had chosen to laugh it off. Thereafter, she had kept away from the animal.

When Prabha had been a baby, the cat had broken his feeding bottle after getting a whiff of the milk. It had bolted when Mangalakka shouted at it, but its claw inadvertently scratched Prabha's cheek as it made its escape. Luckily, the baby's eye was left unscathed. She had raised such a hue and cry over the near-accident that Shiri had rid the house of the cat. From then on, Mangalakka hadn't allowed any cat in the house.

But now, ever since she returned from Panjim, she had felt so lonely that she didn't even realize when the cat had made itself at home with her. One day, when Mangalakka had begun having her lunch, it had parked itself in front of her. She had even lifted her hand to chase it away, but the cat just turned its head and stared at the lifted hand. The hand came down, automatically, and the cat had remained crouching until Mangalakka finished her meal. It moved only after Mangalakka gave it the fish bones and the last handful of her food. From then on, this unwittingly became the norm. Nobody knew whose the cat was or where it had

come from. It had probably been abandoned, but now it was hers.

Bilu would occasionally raid Mangalakka's stock of fish and steal her milk, but Mangalakka didn't mind any more. People at Prabha's parties drank such a lot of expensive whisky and beer. How much would she lose if the poor cat drank a little milk?

As the monsoons were fast approaching, Mangalakka began preparations to meet it by cleaning and resetting the roof tiles.

Prabha had turned up all of a sudden. His usual routine was a monthly visit – always a Sunday – with Namita. Since he was supposed to go to Mumbai one of these days, he had come for Goan snacks for Daddy. There was sattam, the sweet chewy desiccated jackfruit flakes; solam, the enzyme-rich skins of kokum steeped in its juice; and neerponnos, the Goan breadfruit.

Two men were on the roof and a couple of women on the ground. Mangalakka was engrossed in the work as well, wiping the tiles and handing them over. Prabha didn't look pleased at this scene. "Aiyee, why do you have to work? Couldn't you employ another labourer?"

Whilst leaving, he placed five hundred rupees on the table in front of Mangalakka. "I never knew that there was so much work to be done!" he said in a voice heavy with emotion. "Here, keep this for now. I'll bring more later."

Mangalakka laughed heartily at this foolishness. "I don't need any money from you, Prabha. This plantation gives me all that I want. How do you think I educated you?"

Her voice turned hoarse. "What I want is not your money but for the two of you to be happy." Prabha averted his face and bid her a hasty goodbye. Perhaps his eyes had turned moist too.

She had got through the first monsoon after returning from Panjim. Even the heavy downpours did not break Prabha and Namita's routine of coming to visit her. Yet, never once did they ask, "Aiyee, when are you coming to Panjim?" It wasn't as though Mangalakka would have rushed to obey the summons the moment they called. But her son should have asked. Or was he waiting for his mother to speak first? To offer to come? Mangalakka wondered if she had erred somewhere.

Saturday was some sort of a holiday. Prabha had informed her that they would be coming down for a couple of days. But they hadn't.

Sunday morning, and they still hadn't come. After noon, he came alone. The sprouted moong beans she had cooked with river prawns the day before had already become stale. The realization that her son was slowly becoming alienated from her gnawed at her. She was shrivelling up from inside. Namita hadn't come – perhaps she wouldn't be coming anymore.

Mangala waited in silence. After a few moments, Prabha said, "Aiyee, you haven't even asked why Namita isn't here."

She didn't speak a word. Perhaps it was the smell of the soured lentils. Or the disappointment that they hadn't turned up. She felt sick.

"Aiyee, Namita's soon to give you a grandchild!"

The freshness of a splash of spring water on her face. A sunburst of joy filled her to overflowing. It was as though a great weight had been lifted off her chest.

She was so overcome with happiness that she didn't know what to do. Once she had asked the customary queries of "How is she? Which month is she in?" her mill cranked into action. She recited a whole checklist of how Namita had to be cared for and what she ought and ought not to eat: "Don't let her eat papaya or cashewnuts; don't leave the house at nights; don't keep late nights; no jumping about and no falls –"

Prabha began to laugh, interrupting the never-ending list. "I wouldn't be able to remember all this, Aiyee. She's just in her third month. You can tell her all this in person. I'm bringing Namita next month."

Mangalakka waited anxiously for the month to end. Her daughter-in-law must be in the throes of duvalle, the pregnant woman's craving for some favourite dish. What would she want? Pickles? She made breadfruit papads, karmallam lonnchem pickle and shevya-ghons, those deeppfried vermicelli-like extrusions of gram paste.

And finally, Namita did come. Silently, she took in Mangalakka's array of goodies. After what seemed a long time, Prabha cleared his throat. "Aiyee, she just doesn't feel like eating anything."

"That's only to be expected. But something at least –"

"She feels like eating butter-chicken." Prabha's tone was supportive.

"But meat heats up the body," Mangalakka's voice betrayed deep concern. "It's not advisable for pregnant women."

"The doctor said I could eat meat." Namita's voice was cool.

Mangalakka's enthusiasm was waning. Whilst going back, Prabha took only the ghons, because he loved the dish. She had hoped that this time at least, Prabha would call her to Panjim. However, he didn't bring up the topic right until the end. Should I have considered their needs, she wondered. Should I have offered to go with them myself?

Bilu twisted on the bed, and her sleep was disturbed. She opened her eyes and glanced at her feet. The cat curled into a ball, was yawning luxuriantly. Dawn was spreading its light over the sky, and the first sunbeams were probing through the gaps in the roof tiles. Mangalakka hurriedly got up and began her chores.

She had almost finished when the sun came up the horizon. She filled the rice pot and went down to the orchard to gather some firewood to get the fire going.

Madhav-bhat, who was walking along the footpath above, called out to her. "Hello there Mangalakka, I have heard that Shiri is coming. Is it true?"

Shiri. The name made her start. When the context dawned on her, she was overjoyed. "There are still a couple of months to go. She has just in her seventh month."

The thought that Shiri would be coming sent the blood surging through her aging veins. She would massage her

grandson with oil, bathe him, play with him. She would hold Shiri in her arms! Mangalakka was lost in a reverie. She breezed through her chores for the rest of the day, her heart as light as a feather.

When she woke up from a short nap in the afternoon, her neighbour Rukmini came calling. "So Prabha hasn't come today either, has he?"

Mangalakka's senses went on alert. For the last one year, she's been trying to ferret out details from me. She has sniffed that relations between mother and daughter-in-law aren't exactly humming. And so, whenever Mangalakka met Rukmini, she made it a point to praise her daughter-in-law. She hasn't come to express her worries that Prabha hasn't turned up, she mused. She's come to pity me because my son has stopped visiting!

"But how can he?" Mangalakka said, in a worried voice. "He just wrote to say that Namita has been advised three months of rest. She's not supposed to move at all!" "What sort of pregnancies are these?" Rukmini shook her head. "In our time, we were told that exercise is good and we were made to work hard."

"That's because we were used to our difficult chores. Today's girls are more delicate – Namita just isn't used to hard work. She was married as soon as she finished her studies. I'm so worried about how they'll manage now."

"And so you should be! In fact, I'm quite surprised that you have come to stay here – it isn't as though you have to be here, because, you know, some small loss could be tolerated. Of course, it isn't for me to comment about what's between you people, but I would have thought that you'd be needed there more. Don't you agree?"

Rukmini has hit the nail on the head. I long to be there too. But how can I tell her that?

She changed the subject, talking at length about how the betelnut plantation had suffered while she was away in Panjim, how the water channels had silted up and how the hut along with the firewood inside had been reduced to a termite colony –

"Oh my, it's past five." Rukmini got up hurriedly. "There's a good film on TV today. Why don't you come and watch TV at our place, instead of sitting at home? They say the movie's really good."

"I'm too old to watch films –"

"Wouldn't it be better to watch TV than sitting alone at home, worrying about your daughter-in-law? TV will be a distraction. Come on!"

In any case, Prabha won't be coming now, she decided. Whatever's been cooked is enough for tonight. Seems ungracious to turn down Rukmini's insistent invitation too. Mangalakka got up.

The usual Hindi masala. Rich girl meets poor boy; they fall in love; they quarrel; they make up; they want to get married; opposition from both families; lots of fighting in between; a little humour; they get married despite opposition; begin a new home; pregnancy; problems of a home without elders; mother frets over her children's problems and comes rushing to their aid; mother, son and daughter-in-law live happily ever

after. It meandered on for a long time, with goons and cops in between. Mangalakka: however, had pressed her mental pause button in the scene where son, mother and daughter-in-law united. The scene played itself over and over again before her mind's eye. Halting the rickshaw at the door, Mangalakka steps down and enters the bungalow. Namita is sleeping in the bedroom, Prabha is sitting on the bed, distraught and the whole house is a mess. They see Mangalakka, and are overwhelmed with relief and happiness.

Tears rolled down Mangalakka's eyes.

"What happened, Mangalakka? Did the film move you so?" asked Rukmini's daughter.

Still in her reverie, Mangalakka returned home. She switched on the kitchen light. She had lost her appetite, but could not abide the thought of wasting good food. A curry pot polished clean and an emptied rice-container greeted her. Bilu was stretched our in the hearth.

Furious, she picked up a log of wood and brandished it at the animal, intent on teaching it a lesson. Then she paused to look again. The cat's stomach was bulging. A little too much for just one heavy meal.

So that's the reason for those nightly absences. She pushed the stick back into the fireplace and began to stroke the eat's pregnant belly.

When she had first returned from Panjim, she could never sleep till after midnight. That, of course, resulted in her getting up late. Later, the pattern had reversed itself. At twilight, her eyelids started drooping, and before the break of dawn, when it was still dark outside, she woke up. But today was different.

She simply couldn't sleep. When Bilu curled up at her feet, she drew the quilt over the cat and immersed herself in thought, stroking the animal absently.

I shouldn't have stood on my pride this way - after all, Prabha is my own son. As much steeped in self-respect as I. He must be waiting this very instant, for me to come back to him, on my own. It wasn't as if he chased me out of his house. It was I who came away. How can I expect him to call me back, then? I should know, more than anyone else, that this certainly isn't the time to sit down with a checklist and try to calculate if the fault was his or mine. My grandchild will enter this world painlessly only if I take care of my daughter-in-law. Namita is going to give birth to my own progeny. My time with my grandchild will provide a purpose to my old age. Give some meaning to my endless days. Namita needs me today. When she goes into the throes of labour, she will need me close by to lend her strength and courage. I should have gone days ago – I have made a great mistake.

Her eyes fell on the cat as soon as she rose. A ripple of unease went through her. Who will take care of Bilu? That's to say, if I go at all!

She worked with a light heart the whole day, but a decision eluded her.

Shenvtu had been called to husk the betelnuts, and she came in rather early. "Can I come tomorrow? Mangaldas has called me today. They're going to Panjim tomorrow."

"Panjim?" the question popped out of her mouth before she could stop herself. Prabna's Panjim!

"Haven't you heard? Mangaldas and his wife are going to America. To visit their son."

After getting Mangalakka's consent, Shenvru left. Mangalakka went about her daily chores, trying to while away the time. Around eleven, the fishermonger called out. She wouldn't have bought any fish today, but now she would have to buy some for Bilu's sake. She saw Mangaldas Acharya near Ananth's Temple, when she reached the road with the pan for fish. By the time the fishermonger filled the pan from the basket tied to his bicycle, Mangaldas had reached her.

She opened the conversation casually. "I heard that you're going to America. Is it true?"

"Absolutely!" Mangaldas's face was glowing with excitement. "Our daughter-in-law is expecting. They want the mother to be close at the time of delivery, so our son is sending the tickets. We have got this chance to go only because of our grandchild – or else, we couldn't even have dreamt of seeing America!"

She tried hard to hide the turmoil within. "Which month is your daughter-in-law in?"

"The sixth month. There's still a month and a half for us to go, but we have to get our passports and complete the other formalities. That's why we are going to Panjim tomorrow. I had just gone to engage Jose Filipe's cab."

Here's a mother going to America all the way from

Loliem, to be with her daughter-in-law at the time of her delivery. Can't I go from Loliem to Panjim?

They want the mother to be close by at the time of delivery. Mangaldas's words kept churning within her, as she entered the house. Even before she reached the open razangann, her mind was made up. She would go to Panjim. Tomorrow.

Mangalakka set about the task of closing the house. She even forfeited her afternoon rest. In the evening, she went to Mangaldas Acharya's home.

"I just came to ask, you're going to Panjim tomorrow, will there be place for one more person? Of course, I don't want to inconvenience you."

Mangaldas was delighted at her request. "There's no need to be so apologetic. And don't worry, I'll take you straight to your son's house!"

Since Shenvtu was working there, Mangalakka informed her that she needn't come over the next day. At home, she instructed Sanvllo to look after the orchard as usual, asked him to feed Bilu at least once a day, and began to pack her belongings.

She ate a little less than usual that night, in order to feed the cat well. She didn't sleep well. Nevertheless, she woke up at dawn. Taking care to get out of bed without disturbing the sleeping Bilu, she made tea and then, had a wash with cold water. She picked up her idols, wrapped them in the sacred silk cloth and packed them in the bag. Then, placing the leftover milk in the eat's saucer, Mangalakka closed the house.

Mangaldas and his wife were both very talkative. They chattered away to her incessantly, throughout the journey. Mostly about their son, a little about their daughter-in-law and their forthcoming trip to America.

Mangalakka began to feel lighter, as though a great burden had been lifted from her chest. Prabha may not express it outwardly, perhaps, but he would definitely be relieved. And Namita - it was at this time that she was most in need of a woman's support. I will take care of her every need, so the remaining months will go by easily. And then – then Shiri will come. I will massage him with oil, bathe him, play with him, hold him in my arms!

Despite her protests, Mangaldas dropped her right on Prabha's doorstep. Choked as she was with emotion, Mangalakka didn't even invite them in. She even forgot to thank them!

The door opened before she could ring the bell. Prabha stood on the doorstep, ready to leave for the office. His surprise at her arrival was obvious.

"Aiyee! What happened? What brings you here suddenly?"

Was that a slight crease on Prabha's forehead? He seemed a little too stunned at her appearance.

"I was too worried to stay," she explained. "How is Namita?"

By which time somebody asked, "Who is it, Prabha?" His mother-in-law emerged from inside.

They had only met at the wedding and if Prabha had not told her, she would not have known. "This is Namita's mother. You haven't recognized her? Come in." He picked up her bag and led her in. "You don't have to worry at all, Aiyee, now that Namita has her mum to look after her. She'll be here for six whole months."

Mangalakka's enthusiasm congealed into an icy mass.

"Do come in." The mother-in-law stepped forward. "Just this morning, Prabha was saying that we really should go and see you this Sunday. Didn't you, Prabha?"

And Mangalakka entered her son's house like his mother-in-law's guest.

That evening, Prabha came back from his office earlier than usual. "So Aiyee, you'll be staying here for a few days, right?" he asked, sipping his tea.

"Why should 1 stay if I'm not needed?" she wanted to say, but bit back the retort.

"I would have stayed, but the gods are at home," she said in a low voice. "I offered some flowers and incense this morning before I came. I have to be home tomorrow, or I will not be at peace." It was a relief that she remembered to whip out the white lie about the gods.

She didn't remember to ask forgiveness of the idols which were still lying packed in their silken anvallem in her bag.

Brushing aside Prabha's suggestion that they return together on Sunday, she insisted on going home the very next day. Prabha may have thought it demeaning before his mother-in-law to send his mother home by bus, because he instructed the driver to take her home to Loliem by car.

A vast emptiness filled Mangalakka's mind. Her dreams hung in tatters. She had aged twenty four years in the last twenty four hours.

As she entered the house with her bag, a warm miaow greeted her. It was Bilu, rubbing and purring against her legs.

She squatted on the ground and took Bilu in her lap. "Don't you worry now, I'm here," she whispered, and burst into convulsive sobs.

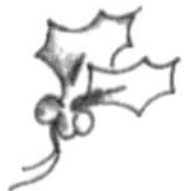

The Divine One

Guru sat in his easy-chair, watching a Goa Doordarshan programme on his black and white TV, when he thought he heard a knock on the door. Premabai was busy with her Friday puja. With one eye on the TV and the other on the laddus in the puja, Vikas and Vimal pretended to do their homework.

Guru wasn't sure whether he had heard a knock on the door or a sound from the TV. He had bought the second-hand television three months ago from his manager on monthly instalments of a hundred and fifty rupees, to be deducted from his salary for a year. The TV worked like a dream for a month, but had started emitting strange noises of late.

Premabai turned her attention from the puja towards the TV. Then she noticed the shut door, and began, "How often do I have to tell you, the front door should be kept open when puja is being offered to Lakshmi. They say that she turns her back on a closed door."

Lakshmi! Over the last thirty years, Guru had grown weary looking for the elusive Goddess of Wealth. How much he had entreated her! He had prayed at temples, roadside shrines, even at pennant-festooned trees and rocks. Hope had all but withered away. But ever since he met Kushaghaddi, the soothsayer, a few tender shoots had sprouted back again on his tree of hope. "Your desire will be fulfilled," the oracle had intoned.

But when?

"Confer peace on the souls of your forefathers by appeasing them with pind-daan," he was told. But how do we recognize the souls of our ancestors, wondered Guru. On Father's last death anniversary, the crow had not eaten the pind, the obligatory offering for the dead. After this incident, Guru had taken the trouble of placing the offering on the roof every new-moon night.

On his last visit to Kusha, he was told not to presume that a soul would necessarily come in the form of a crow. It could assume the form of any creature.

There was a sound at the door, again. Who could it be?

He was about to ask Vikas to open the door, but seeing the children engrossed in their books and recalling Premabai's words about Lakshmi's tendency to skip closed doors, Guru got up from the easy chair, asking, "Who's there?"

There was no response.

Premabai, who had just finished her puja, turned around. "Go and see, at least!" her eyes seemed to say.

He unlatched the door, and was dumbstruck by the regal appearance and proud demeanour of his visitor.

The children's eyes, which had turned from their homework to the TV, were now riveted to the door. Premabai, who had got up with the little tray of puja-blessed gram to serve to the children, also stood gaping.

Without waiting for an invitation, the dog walked in as if it were his own house, and nestled down smartly in the easy chair just vacated by Guru.

Once he got over his initial astonishment, Guru began to feel distinctly annoyed. He considered chasing the animal away with the stick in the corner, but paused.

The dog's coat glistened as if he had just had a bath. A white stripe ran down his forehead like a smeared tilak. Guru looked at Premabai, who stared unblinkingly at the animal.

"Looks exactly like the vehicle of Lord Dattatreya, doesn't he?" remarked Guru, glancing at Prema for approval.

"Don't be stupid. Today's Friday, it has to be Lakshmi! Nobody can tell what form she'll take!"

Today had been quite a good day for Guru. This morning, just before going to office, he had gone to check the result of the lottery draw and had been pleasantly surprised to learn that he had won ten rupees on the terminacao. The last two digits of his coupon matched those on the prize-winning ticket. Since Friday was the day of the goddess of wealth, he had invested the entire windfall on ten more lottery tickets. The office closed at six o'clock, but by the time he had finished shutting the windows and locking the doors, it was six thirty. On his way home, when he saw Shiva at the sweet shop, Guru thought of buying some sweets for the children, but had no money to spare.

"Hello, Shiva! Got a bonus today?" he asked.

"No such luck, man. I'm shopping for the boss."

My job's better than his, thought Guru. Both were office peons but Shiva's boss made him run personal errands too, in addition to his messenger's duties at the office. Pondering idly over this comparison, Guru went his own way.

He was anxious to share the news of his minor lottety luck with Premabai, but knew how she would react. "You spent the ten rupees on more lottery tickets? Couldn't you have bought tickets worth two rupees and something for the children with the rest?" Which reminded him that Premabai had told him to buy gram for Friday's puja.

He went back to the market and bought gram for two rupees. With the Margao municipal garden to his left, he climbed up the slope of Yarde Valaulikar Road, looked to the left and right before crossing the street. Cars sped past while he waited for a lull in the traffic.

Suddenly, he noticed something at his feet.

It looked like one of those mithai boxes from the sweet shop. Should he pick it up, or shouldn't he? By this time, another line of cars had begun to speed their way past him. Guru bent furtively and picked up the box. He quickly crossed the road, and walked to the farther end.

A nagging thought pricked at his mind – what if someone had stuffed the box full of trash and thrown it away? He shifted the box from one hand to the other and sniffed at his hand. The fresh aroma of sweetmeats wafted into his nostrils. When he reached the path through the bushes, Guru opened the box and peeked inside. Sweet boondi laddus!

Quickening his pace, Guru climbed over the lower ledge of Monte Hill and then stepped over the upper one into his house.

"I won ten rupees in the Goa lottery today!" he announced enthusiastically, giving the gram and the mithai box to Prema. The children would feast on the sweets for days. He called out to them.

"What's the hurry?" Premabai protested. "I'll put it aside for Friday's puja, first. Gram is our usual offering. Today, we'll offer something sweet as well."

Prema's practical idea of honouring God and satisfying the children alike appealed to him. He had a wash, shut the front door and eased himself into the chair in front of the TV. By this time, Premabai had begun the puja. And now all of sudden this –

It had to be the Goddess, in the form of a dog. Look at

the way he's just walked in and sat down as if it were his by right. And his haughty manner! When Guru sits on that easy-chair, there's just enough room for Vimal to squeeze in beside him. But this dog really filled it up!

When Guru's father sat on the chair too – hey, wait a minute! Could it be Father, come in the form of a dog? It could well be. Guru had been all of fourteen when his father died. Father had suffered a paralytic stroke that left his mouth palsied, unable to speak. He would try to speak, but no one could understand him.

Fifty years ago, it seems, the broad strip of land all the way up to Monte Hill had belonged to Father. Perhaps it was the rise in real estate prices, or perhaps the need for money was too great, but Father had sold the entire property. They say he got a lot of money for it. Some insist that he wasted it all on gambling, but Mother would always maintain that Father had bought gold bars with the money and buried the treasure in a secret place. He used to unearth them one by one whenever he needed money. But he had never told anybody where it was.

It was quite possible. Nobody deposited their money in banks those days. But shouldn't the man have told Mother at least? He had been twisting his mouth as he lay dying, trying to say something. He lay on his deathbed for twenty seven days and finally died with the secret locked up in his heart.

Could he have come now in the form of this dog? Guru folded his palms respectfully.

The bewildered children, who had huddled close, saw

their father with folded palms and sprang up. Premabai picked up the little tray of gram again. She moved ahead gently, and stopped in front of the dog. Then she hesitated, wondering if she should keep the tray in front of him, or put some gram in her hand and take it to his mouth. What if he bit her hand? In that case, it was a dog. Otherwise it was Lakshmi, no doubt!

Premabai hastily poured some gram into her hand and held them near the dog's mouth.

The children held their breath. Guru admired his wife's courage. Premabai brought her hand closer. "Revered Goddess!" she murmured. "Please accept our devout offerings."

But the dog was unmoved. When the gram was brought closer to his snout, he simply turned his head away.

"If we have offended Thee in any way, please forgive us," Premabai knelt before the dog. "Devi, we are thy ignorant children. We do not know what thy desires are." And then looking at Guru, she pleaded, "Please say something at least."

The dog's distinctive pose, the way Premabai knelt and entreated, his own posture with bowed head and folded palms – Guru could almost feel the ambience of Kushaghaddi's den. He was humbled.

"Prema, hurry up, light some incense and bring them here. Bring the vermilion too," he rattled off orders. "Vikas, bring a flower from the hibiscus plant, hurry! Even a bud will do. Vimal, light the oil lamp and bring it here." Having instructed everybody, Guru folded his palms and sat cross-legged on the floor.

Guru had nurtured dreams of riches ever Since his childhood. He believed that happiness lay in money. Some day, he would find the treasure buried by his father, he was sure. Within a couple of years of his father's death, their financial condition had become so dire that he had no option but to drop out of school and look for work. A government job in Panjim was his for the asking but Guru wasn't willing to move out from his house in Margao. Lest his father's buried treasure fall in some stranger's hands, Guru preferred to take whatever job he could get in Margao. He had worn out his sandals going to countless seers and fortune-tellers. Half his earnings were spent on them. But Guru was a persistent man, and to add to this, the woman he had married was very devout. Her influence had nurtured his belief in the spiritual and the supernatural. He had run through the whole gamut of practitioners of the occult. He had tried rice-grain diviners and trance-masters. He had gone to Belgaum and even tried to speak to his father through a spiritual medium. He did manage to connect, but Father must have been stricken with paralysis even after death, because nothing that he spoke was intelligible.

Somebody had told him of Kusha-ghaddi quite recently. Guru made a special trip to the port town of Vasco-da-Gama to see him. Kusha's witchcraft must have been very potent, for people came to see him from distant places. And his clientele wasn't restricted to the poor and the destitute, as the rows of cars parked outside his house testified. Guru's drooping hopes were awakened.

Two weeks ago, on a Friday evening like this, Kusha had intoned amidst shamanical swaying, "Hah, hah, your forefathers hover around you – hah, hah, their blessings are upon you, hah, hah – they speak to you in signs, hah, hah – they are trying to reach you, hah, hah – but you are an ignorant child, hah, hah – be watchful, hah – provide the souls of your ancestors with timely offerings – hah, don't starve them, hah, hah – your problems will be solved, hah, hah, hah!"

His faith had grown by leaps and bounds, and he carried the petals given by Kusha as a talisman in his pocket. "My beloved ancestors, please forgive me. I will make my offering of pind due to you on the next new moon. And let me know if anything more is to be given. But please, understand what is troubling my mind and show me the way."

Vimal lit the lamp and placed it in front of the dog. Vikas brought in a drooping red hibiscus. Premabai lit the incense sticks. When she applied vermilion to his forehead, the dog closed his eyes gently and with great understanding, submitted himself to the ritual. Placing the niranjan in the tray, Premabai extended the sacred lamp, working it in circles round him. With that, Guru could sense a holy aura in the room.

All of a sudden, the dog began to bark loudly. The children almost jumped out of their skins. Premabai quickly joined her hands in supplication. Guru was trying to fathom the reason for the outburst. The dog was staring at the TV.

"Of course! The TV!" Nobody had realized that the TV had been on, all this time. "Vikas, quick, turn it off."

Vikas did so happily, flashing a triumphant glance at Vimal, for Guru never let anyone else touch the television set. But Vimal's focus was on the laddus in the puja corner.

With the TV off, peace pervaded the room. Vimal broke it by turning to his mother. "May we eat the laddus, Mama?"

"You kids think of nothing but eating!" grumbled Premabai as she got up. The moment she lifted the box of sweets, the room resounded with loud barking.

Guru was perplexed. He couldn't understand what his forefather was saying! Nevertheless, he tried to decipher the signals.

Shwan-maharaj, the Dog-Lord, perked up his ears. His neck stiffened and he sniffed hard. Premabai hurried over to the Lord's side with the box of laddus. "Yes, indeed! First bite to the deity." She took a laddu and proffered it to the Goddess. In a trice the laddu from her palm had been gobbled up. Guru was deeply impressed with his wife's adroitness.

"The spirits of our forefathers have now received their nourishment," he intoned.

The white stripe running down the dog's forehead looked like a tilak more than ever, standing out prominently, with the dab of vermilion on it.

"Listen to my entreaties at least now, dear god, revered forefathers – " Guru wasn't really sure if he was petitioning to his forefathers or the god, but he prayed with all the faith he could muster.

Premabai had barely turned around with the box, intending to give laddus to the children, when the dog let off another thunderous volley.

"It's food for the gods. How can just one be enough? Offer him one more."

God gobbled up the second one too.

"Now at least, dear god ... " Guru began. The dog blinked at Guru. Guru felt as though the dog was telling him to wait for a while.

When the third fusillade of barking broke out, Premabai extended the entire box to the Goddess. Even Guru could hear the children swallowing hard.

"Kneel down," he rebuked the children. The two boys prostrated themselves.

When the dog had wolfed down the last laddu, Guru said, "Now bring the gram." As Premabai brought in the little tray of gram, Maharaj stood up. He bounded down from the easy-chair and with a final sweeping look at everybody, went towards the door.

He walked out with a purposeful stride.

Premabai interpreted, "He seems to be asking you to follow him."

Guru was in his vest and pyjama. But Maharaj was beckoning; there was no time to change clothes. Guru leapt up and ran out, grabbing a shirt hanging on the peg.

"It's dark, take Vikas with you." Premabai called out from the doorway.

"No, I'm going alone. Stay inside, I'll come home when

everything is done." So saying, Guru ran after the dog. He was prepared to go wherever Maharaj led him.

Peering through the dark from the doorway, Premabai sent along a silent prayer and gently shut the door.

Maharaj would lead him either towards the top of the hill or the back of his house, Guru thought, but it didn't quite happen that way. With a regal wag of his tail, the dog set off like a true king.

Stepping down from the ledge, he came to the pathway by the bushes. Climbing up, he started walking along the road. Guru followed him with a thumping heart. As they neared the bungalow of Motilal Seth, a bell tinkled and a cycle braked to a halt behind him. "To-m-m-y!"

With one look at the cyclist, the dog bounded off and raced inside Motilal's gate.

Panting hard, the cyclist dismounted.

"What happened, Shiva?" a confused Guru asked, recognizing the cyclist.

"I have roamed all over Margao looking for Sethji's dog. We poor folks have no money to even buy our food grains from the ration shop, but these rich people's dogs are better off than us! When he comes home every evening, my boss gives his dog boondi laddus to eat. We didn't have any sweets in the house today, so I was told to go and buy half a kilo of laddus. The box must have fallen off the cycle carrier when I was returning. I didn't want to get screamed at by the boss, so I went back and bought another box of laddus with my own money. But when I returned to the boss's house, the dog wasn't there. Sethji's wife sent me in search of him. I'm exhausted after searching everywhere, I tell you. I was just going to tell them to lodge a missing-dog complaint with the police when all of a sudden this fellow tears through the bungalow gate in front of my eyes!"

Guru looked beyond the gate. Tommy trotted towards the porch and went round and round in a circle. He lifted a hind leg, irrigated the pillar liberally and without a backward glance, entered the house and disappeared from view.

Guru turned back, feeling as though he had been peed upon.

The Undeserving

Packed like sardines in the Margao-bound bus, Gloria found herself at one end and Neela at the other. They could breathe a little easier at Santacruz, bur Neela was still far away.

This rush was normal as commuters hurried home from work, but having someone to chat with helped kill time and forget the discomfort of travel. Today, as soon as the bus pulled into the Panjim bus stand, Gloria had jumped in behind the driver's cab, and even managed to reserve a sear for Neela. But her friend had got stranded in the aisle in the mad stampede and was propelled to the rear, while a crowd gathered around Gloria.

By the time they reached Agacaim, the crowd had thinned a bit. "Dirty fellow!" Neela muttered under her breath as she made her way towards Gloria. "Lecher!" She was livid with anger.

"Who are you talking about?"

"That baldie over there, the drunken sod!" she pointed.

Gloria looked at the man, who was obviously wearing a wig and who had now found another victim to lean on.

She could instantly recognize men who pawed women in crowded buses, and managed to steer clear of them. And if any man were to touch her even by accident, all she had to do was glower at him and he would move away.

"Why didn't you shove him away?" Gloria asked.

"Filthy idiot! I pushed him. I was angry. But he kept falling on me. Drink brings out the beast in them!"

By this time, the bus was crossing Cortalim bridge. At the next junction, Gloria waved Neela goodbye, got down and looked at her watch. It was a quarter to seven, a little later than usual. She finished work at the bank by five in the evening, but by the time she caught the bus and reached home, it would be six fifteen to six thirty. In any case, what was the point of going home early? If only Glen were here now ... In fact, Glen was due to arrive one of these days. She was eagerly awaiting his call.

Walking towards her home, she caught a glimpse of

someone seated in their balcao and quickened her step, wondering who it might be. Could it be ... ? Yes, it was! It was Glen!

Surprise gave way to a leaping heart. She was alive, alive, with love and happiness. She rushed up the steps.

"Glen! Glen, when did you come? Why didn't you call me?"

"Came around noon. Via Bombay," Glen replied laconically from his seat. "I couldn't get the direct Kuwait-Goa flight."

She took his hand in hers and clasped it tight. 'I'm so happy Glen, so happy!" She wanted him to jump up, take her in his arms and whirl her around. She wanted to twine her hand around Glen's neck and hug him. But he still sat on in his chair – and she felt disappointment fill her.

"C'mon, let's go inside," she pulled him by the hand.

He got up and let himself be led into the bedroom. Once inside, the years of their separation melted in a jiffy, and Gloria couldn't hold herself back any longer. She hugged him tight, nuzzling her head against his shoulder and nibbled at him gently. Suddenly, a sob escaped her. The next moment, before the puzzled Glen could register anything, she laughed happily, "Glen I love you, I love you!"

Normally, Gloria would come home and flop on the bed after a tired day's work. But today, she floated on cloud nine. If she stretched her arms, she thought, she would fly!

"Glen, there's no fish in the house today. Shall we go to the ferry-point and buy some?"

“I asked him,” his mother interjected even before he could answer, “but he said he was too tired. He said rice with curry and pickle would do. He wants to go to bed early.”

Poor Glen must have had a sleepless night. The Kuwait plane was a night flight, and it must have been dawn by the time the Customs clearance was completed.

“You must be exhausted,” Gloria said solicitously.

“I didn’t sleep a wink and to make matters worse, the Goa flight came in late,” Glen grumbled.

“Come on, let’s open the suitcases.” Gloria was naturally anxious to see what Glen had brought her.

There was a knock on the door just as the first suitcase was opened. Glen’s friend Dominic had come to see him. He lingered on for over an hour.

By the time their visitor finally left, Glen was yawning. “I’m very sleepy. Let’s eat quickly. We’ll check the bags tomorrow, Gloria.”

Tomorrow! “Glen, I have got to go to the bank tomorrow.”

“Bunk work,” was Glen’s prompt response.

“How can I? I have got the cash safe keys with me. But I could do one thing – hand over the keys and submit a leave note.”

“Why go all the way to Panjim and come back? You might as well work the whole day,” was his practical suggestion.

“Not a bad idea. In that case, I’ll apply for leave from the day after tomorrow, okay?”

“Suit yourself. But let’s eat, quick. I can’t even keep my eyes open.” And in truth, Glen’s eyelids were heavy with sleep.

Gloria set out the plates, rice and curry hurriedly, taking special care to serve him the mackerel para that she had been saving for Glen. He shovelled in his food, went into the bedroom after dinner and promptly fell asleep.

My Glen, mused Gloria. Gone after twenty five days of marriage, and back after two long years. He's just come home and was with his mother the whole evening. She couldn't help but feel a twinge of envy for Mai, her mother-in-law. Why, even Dominic was luckier than her. Glen had spoken with him for quite a while.

She shook off the buzzing thoughts and prepared to sleep, but her mind, caught in a maze of emotions, kept sleep at bay.

She turned to look at Glen. He was sleeping like a baby. He must have been really tired, she reasoned. Otherwise, his excitement would have matched mine. Such a deep slumber, just when their two-year separation had finally come to an end.

That was one thing in favour of life before marriage. Sleep came to you without a fuss. Once you were married, though – oh, but those first twenty five days! Glorious days when Glen wouldn't leave her side even for a moment, when each day by Glen's side had passed in such blissful ecstasy. Matching his excitement, cooling his passion, teasing him, over and over again. And then, all of a sudden, it was back to the dreaded spinsterhood. Separation. Long nights of tossing and turning. Her feelings, imprisoned and suffocated. Her self, denied. Only a flickering flame of hope that this separation would end soon. Today, all those bottled-up feelings were bubbling over. Today, the flame was bursting into life.

But Glen? He was fast asleep, exhausted.

She was irritated with herself. Glen wasn't leaving tomorrow. There was still the day after, and the next week, and a whole month, at the very least!

Stifling a sigh, she turned over. For a fleeting moment, she thought of opening the suitcases to see what Glen had brought her and even sat up, but gave up the idea. She would return from the bank early tomorrow, and then they would go through the bags together. With that thought, she finally fell asleep.

Glen was still asleep next morning as she was getting ready to leave for work. "Glen, wake up," she touched him. "I'm leaving."

"Eh? So early?"

"It's almost nine. I have the safe keys, remember? I can't afford to be late."

"Okay. Bye!" And he turned on his side and went back to sleep.

Gloria bent down, her lips close to his ears. "Sleep to your heart's content now," she whispered. "But tonight, I'm certainly not going to let you sleep!"

Glen smiled dreamily and planted a quick kiss on her hand.

She kept brushing that hand to her cheeks and lips all the way to work. The whole bank saw her flitting like a butterfly as she went about her duties, and knew without being told that Glen had come home. Even the accountant laughingly warned her, "Careful while counting! Should I put someone else at the cash counter?"

But Gloria didn't trip up at the cash counter. Once she had finished balancing her cash, she wrote a leave application, informed everybody that she would be back only on Monday, and left the office early. She didn't meet Neela as she took the four forry-five bus. Though Neela's office was on the way, she skipped it, impatient to rush back home. Once she had found a seat in the bus though, she felt a little prick of guilt. She should have at least to have told her friend that Glen had come home. But it was too late now. At least she managed to grab a seat because she had caught the early bus, she reasoned. Then she groaned inwardly. Why was the bus taking so long?

Finally, she got down at her stop in Cortalim. When she entered the house, she found Glen sprawled in front of the TV.

"Just in time! A surprise for you!" Glen announced enthusiastically.

Nothing seemed different, she thought, as she walked in. But – wait a moment.

"Video!" Glen proclaimed proudly. "Now you can watch a movie every day!"

She was thrilled. A video was something that they really needed. Even their neighbour Minguelina had one. "It's beautiful," she murmured as she ran her fingers admiringly over the VCR. "Thank you Glen!" If Mai hadn't been hovering behind, she would have kissed him.

She stepped into the bedroom. Hmm, Glen's suitcases had already been emptied. Mai perhaps?

"Glen, who unpacked the suitcases?"

"I did. I had to get the video out, right?" Glen brushed aside her question. "Look at what I brought you!" He threw open the wardrobe and an array of goodies stared back at her – two expensive sarees, dress materials, a bracelet watch, a hand-embroidered purse, a make-up set, some vials of perfume and a deodorant spray. Gloria's eyes glistened at the sight of the gifts. Then, her hands touched two big bottles.

"That's Black Label whisky," Glen said. "I bought them at the duty free shop."

"For me?" Mischief glinted in her eyes.

"For your husband," Glen countered.

A Hindi movie was played on the VCR before dinner. Just then, their neighbour Peter dropped in with his wife. They sat down too, and watched the film.

The movie was typically long. Past eleven, Gloria had had enough of the movie. Then again, she couldn't very well say, "You folks carry on, we're turning in." So she was forced to sit out the movie till its end.

She quickly clamped a hand on Glen's mouth when he yawned as soon he hit the mattress. "Don't say you're feeling sleepy tonight too, I'm warning you!"

"It's very late," he laughed, "that's why I yawned."

"You slept like a log last night, but I didn't sleep a wink. Tonight I won't let you sleep!"

And indeed, she teased him, cuddled him, wrenched

him within her embrace, and she wouldn't let him sleep for over an hour. Glen was exhausted.

"Glen! Is that it?" Gloria's disappointment was palpable.

"Yes. The show's over. Now I'm going to sleep. You sleep too." And without further ado, he fell asleep.

Reasoning that the two-year hiatus between their twenty fifth and twenty sixth night probably accounted for his exhaustion, she gave in to the arms of sleep.

An idea occurred to her in the morning. They would go to Old Goa, and visit the shrine of Goa's Patron Saint. She shook Glen awake. "Glen, wake up!"

"It's Juma today," came Glen's sleepy murmur. "We sleep on holidays."

"You're not in Kuwait, Glen! Friday's a working day here. Get up, lazybones! We're going to Old Goa."

Were they to stay at home, she was afraid that either someone would come to see Glen or he himself might go off to visit somebody. She wouldn't have to share Glen with anybody if they went out together.

She kept talking to him all the way. About home, about the village, about her work – just about anything and everything.

After praying at the relics of St Francis Xavier, they went to Margao, where they lunched at Longuinhos.

"Shall we go for a movie?" Gloria suggested enthusiastically.

"A movie? We have a video now, don't we?" He made her suggestion sound silly.

"Let's go to the Colva beach then, shall we?"

"Oh no, my dear, I'm sleepy and tired. Let's go back."

It dawned on Gloria just then, that Glen was growing old. He was greying at the temples, and the old fire had dimmed too.

She was quiet and pensive all the way home, but he didn't even notice. If anything, her silence let him snooze throughout the journey.

Once they reached home, Gloria surveyed herself critically in the mirror. A faint trace of a line creased her forehead. Or was that her imagination? Nor a single hair had greyed so far, but it probably wouldn't be long before some appeared. And that glow on her face was fast disappearing too.

Time waits for no one. Their marriage had been a late one to begin with – she was past thirty and Glen had been thirty eight. Forty today. Two whole years had passed between the twenty fifth and the twenty sixth days of their togetherness. And at the end of this month's holiday of Glen's, two more years of their life would be gone. Two years before the next holiday.

No, I won't allow this month to just go by. The body has to be sated. It has to bloom and bear fruit. Or there will be no fulfilment of life.

She went to the market while Glen slept and bought some meat. Flesh aroused the flesh, she had heard.

"Girl, have you forgotten that Friday is a day of abstinence?" Mai asked, exasperated. "Shouldn't you have bought it tomorrow or the day after?" Gloria did not reply.

She put the meat away in the fridge. It could wait a day to be cooked.

At the bell of Angelus, Glen went out with his friends. He was back at dinnertime. He watched TV for a while afterwards, and then promptly lay down to sleep.

Gloria followed him. "Wait for me Glen! I'll change and come in a minute."

"Eh, abstinence today ..." Glen joked sleepily.

"I have abstained for the last two years!" retorted Gloria, slipping into her nightie and switching off the light. "Glen!" she huffed, exasperated. "Are you really sleeping?"

"Yes, my darling. I'm tired. Yesterday was enough, now tomorrow ... good night!" He turned on his side and was asleep in a trice.

She tossed and turned. Thirty five and forty isn't old age, she consoled herself. That bank accountant who had been transferred last year had his first child when he was forty seven. And the wife of Surya, their tenant, gave birth to her seventh child when she was forty!

God is certainly unjust. He gives nothing to those who have none, and to those who already have so many, he gives seven! Some time back, when she had asked Surya's wife, the latter had replied tearfully, "Curse him! He agrees during the day but when he comes home at night, he's drunk and gives me a rough time. He even thrashes me if I refuse!"

Her heart beat a little faster. She pulled the pillow from under her head and hugged it.

Glen was the phlegmatic type, unlike her. Even as a newlywed, it had been a case of thus far and no further. He had had to be thoroughly aroused by Gloria, and had never taken the initiative. She fell asleep, vowing to turn him on the day after.

Gloria laid her plans well the next morning. She cooked Glen's favourite spicy pork sorpotel, salted beef tongue and tender loin steaks. Glen smacked his lips and ate with great relish, and even took a second helping of the sorpotel. She was pleased that he had enjoyed her cooking.

But all in vain. By sundown, Glen had developed such a bad stomach ache that the doctor had to be called.

"The usual gastric trouble," diagnosed the doctor. He injected an anti-spasmodic and prescribed some sleeping pills.

Tossing and turning again that night, she mused ruefully that she should have asked the doctor for some sleeping pills for herself too! She must have finally dozed off around dawn.

When Glen woke up the next day, he found Gloria still asleep, and roused her for Sunday Mass.

"How are you now?" she asked, with some guilt.

"Don't worry, I'm perfectly alright. Slight hitch with the digestive system. No problem now!"

Returning home from Mass, who should they find waiting in the doorway but Neela! Worried that she hadn't met Gloria in three days, she had come to inquire about her. A true friend indeed. She took a look at Gloria's tired eyes and winked. "Well? Glen didn't let you sleep last night, eh?"

Gloria remained silent.

"Have you read today's newspaper?" asked Neela, as they were chatting. "There was a rape case in our neighbourhood yesterday."

"Really?"

"There's an elderly man who stays alone, not far from our house. He's a good man when sober. But when he gets drunk, he turns really ugly. Yesterday he guzzled down litres, went to his neighbour's, and then this dirty business! It's all in the papers."

Surya's wife's words, too, echoed in Gloria's mind: "When they get drunk, you can't reason with them!"

That evening, Glen was preparing to go out when Gloria stopped him. She took him into the room and pointed at the bottle of whisky. "What's this for? Just a display?"

"Of course not, my girl. That's premium scotch – only for a special occasion!"

Without further ado, Gloria seized the bottle and opened it.

"You mean ..." Glen was confused. Normally, Gloria wasn't too happy if he were to drink a little extra.

"Instead of drinking outside, you might as well do so at home," Glotia reasoned.

Glen downed peg after peg, clearly enjoying himself. In between, Gloria brought him some snacks to munch on. Glen drank on till the end of the movie on the video.

Then, she served dinner. By the time he went to bed, Glen had downed another couple of drinks. She snuggled up to Glen. He smiled benignly at her, looking through heavy-lidded eyes. She guided his hands on her body. An obedient Glen moved his fingers slightly, but then, his hands went limp.

Her hands roved all over his body, but Glen was already deep in slumber.

It took a long while for the blood in her heated veins to cool down. By the time the tension eased from her taut body and she could get some sleep, it was well past midnight.

In the morning, Mai knocked on the door to announce that it was eight o'clock, and Gloria woke up. She got ready quickly, but by the time she reached the bus stop, it was already past nine. Thank god she didn't have the safe keys with her!

The bus is always late when you need it most. After more than ten minutes, it finally rumbled up. It was rush hour but the crowd had also multiplied since today was a Monday. Gloria managed to squeeze in somehow.

Until they reached Agacaim market, Gloria wasn't really conscious of the vaguely familiar man trying to lean on her. He tried to paw her, using every slight jolt of the bus to slouch on her. Her irritation mounted. She hadn't been in the best of moods to begin with. And now this sick lecher!

When the man leaned on her again at the next turn, she

turned to scorch him with an angry stare. Yes, it was the same idiot who had troubled Neela the other day. Reeking of liquor, he leered at her furious glance.

The smell was nauseating. Odd, this business with liquor – how it inflamed some! In vain she had sought its help last night. Instead, here it was, accosting her this morning.

The bus screeched to a halt and the man promptly pressed against her again. She exploded in fury, slamming her bag on the man's head with all her might. "You dirty boozard, drinking and falling on women! Lean on me again and I'll smash your face!"

Without waiting to collect his wig, which had been dislodged by the blow of Gloria's bag, the man hurriedly got down at the next stop and disappeared.

Avoiding the curious stares of other passengers, Gloria choked back a sob, longing desperately for the journey to end.

The Sizzle And The Fizzle

Caetano's wedding! Menino alias Minu stepped down from the taxi with Bella. The wedding hall was decked up with streamers and decorations. Minu glanced at Bella. The pale blue gown flattered her slender figure; her face glowed like a rose. Minu felt gratified that his suit too, tailored for their wedding, fitted him perfectly.

When they entered the hall, they were immediately surrounded by people – more girls than boys – and cries of "Hi Handsome!"

Bella couldn't help wondering if the girls weren't being a little too enthusiastic. The jokes grew wittier by the minute.

The bride and groom cut their wedding cake. After the ceremonial toast, everybody clinked wine glasses and drank to the health and happiness of the newly married couple. The groom's younger sister Filomena, nicknamed Fulambai, came around followed by the steward with a tray of drinks.

"Hello Menino, what will you have? A whisky?"

"That would be nice, thank you."

"And you, ma'am?"

"No, thanks."

Menino urged her, "C'mon, just have one."

"You must have a drink, ma'am. A beer?"

"Go on," insisted Menino.

Bella accepted a glass. "You know," she hissed into his ear, "I prefer not to drink."

"You can start now," Minu proclaimed expansively, taking a swig of whisky from his glass.

A month and a half ago, they had gone on their honeymoon to Bangalore. Minu was talkative by nature, but Bella was quite reserved. At first, Minu had thought that she was shy in company, but discovered that she wasn't any different even when they were alone, together.

"Say something!"

"What do you want me to say?"

"I have been talking away for a whole hour, and you've been quiet all the time. Say something at least. I'm fed up of listening to my own voice."

"Minu, that's just how I am. Go on talking, I'm not bored."

They had strolled into a restaurant.

"But I don't drink, Minu."

"Relax, sweetheart. A beer is harmless."

"No, Minu, please. You can go ahead, I'll have a soft drink."

But he insisted on ordering for both of them. Bella silently lifted the glass to her mouth.

"Don't tell me you've never had a drink?" he asked.

With a quiet smile, Bella nodded her head.

"Beer isn't really a drink, you know. It's just like water."

She smiled in agreement.

"Don't call me a drunkard, but personally, I prefer whisky. That's what I drink whenever I sit down for a round with friends. Beer's too mild – not a drink at all."

Bella opened her mouth at last. "You're right."

"You've never had a whisky, have you?"

"Of course not. Even a beer goes to my head. Imagine what would happen if I had whisky."

"Really? Beer gives you a kick?"

"Well, not a kick. But it affects me."

Minu's eyebrows shot up. "Surprising!"

The drink was finished, and a fresh beer replaced the empty glass.

Bella started reminiscing. "The first time I ever had a drink was when I went to Mumbai. That was about five years ago. Uncle gave us all beer to drink. I had mine and then – " The memory made her smile, and she burst into laughter. "Can you imagine it? I even sang a song right in front of everyone there! Beer must have made me bold." She laughed so much that tears came to her eyes. Minu found himself chuckling along with her.

People from other tables began to stare at them, but his eyes were on her. This was the first time that he was seeing Bella talk and laugh in such a carefree way. She looked so pretty when she laughed. He could listen to her all day, he thought.

Bella talked incessantly all the way from the restaurant to their hotel. It was a thoroughly enjoyable evening.

"Minu, did I bore you yesterday?" she whispered as he opened his eyes the next morning.

"Of course not. Why?"

She hesitated for a moment. "All that beer," she said, ruefully. "I must have spoken too much."

"You didn't speak anything out of the way. You were perfectly normal."

"Thanks, but are you being honest? Or are you just trying to please me?"

"No, sweetheart," he assured her. "I mean it." He drew her close.

"Why didn't you speak anything, then? Last night, I was the only one doing the talking!" said Bella, nudging him away gently.

"And I was listening!"

But Bella wasn't convinced. Minu explained, "Frankly, once I have a drink, I cannot talk."

"But why?"

"I don't know! Normally I talk a lot. But when I drink, I clam up."

"But, you said that you normally drink whisky. We only had beer!"

"It's just that whenever I have a drink, my tongue seems to freeze. My head is absolutely clear. But my tongue .,."

"Bur why?"

"Last night, did the beer make you drunk?"

"No ..."

"But you were so garrulous!"

"..."

"That's just it! There isn't a reason for it."

That evening too, Bella had talked animatedly over drinks at dinner. Minu had listened with rapt attention. It had been another lovely evening.

The dance was announced, Minu hurriedly gulped down his whisky. "Come on! Drink up!"

Taking a couple of quick sips, Bella left the beer glass on the table and joined Minu as they walked to the dance floor.

"Minu, we'll go home early okay?"

"We'll play it by ear."

"I thought you said that we would go for a movie!"

"I said that if we weren't having a good time we could think of the cinema."

"If you find good company, you might just forget your own wife!" joked Bella, gently pinching him.

After the dance, they found the drink steward with his

tray standing near their table. Minu picked a whisky for himself and a beer for Bella.

Agnelo, Martin and Joseph stood around, talking animatedly and Minu joined them.

The band struck up. Minu decided to sit out the dance. Agnelo led Bella to the floor.

Minu sipped his drink, waiting for the dance to end. But Bella didn't return to the table immediately. She stood around chatting and laughing uproariously with Agnelo, Peter and the others. Minu finally decided to join Bella.

"Talk of the devil!" said Agnelo. "We were just telling your wife what a Romeo you were! We told her to keep you on a tight leash!"

They all joined in the laughter, including Bella.

Minu wanted to say, That's fine, but why are you flirting with my wife? But the whisky had frozen his tongue.

"Don't worry! He won't get away with it!" Bella remarked with mock severity, sending everybody into fits of laughter.

Minu worried that the beer had affected Bella a bit too much.

The next dance was announced. He wanted to dance this one with Bella, but Katherine buttonholed him and began to talk. The music began, but by the time he had turned around, Bella was already on the floor with somebody. He had to dance with Katherine.

Katherine was a good dancer, but his attention was on Bella. When he missed his step for the second time, Katherine pinched him. "What's wrong Minu? Who are you staring at? You shouldn't have danced with anybody but your wife!"

Bella chose that very moment to look towards Minu, just as he reacted with a start to the tweak. Embarrassed, he opened his mouth to apologize, but the words froze in their tracks.

"It isn't polite to stare when your wife is dancing with somebody else, Minu," teased Katherine. Minu laughed sheepishly and tried to force some life into his dancing. Mercifully, the dance came to an end just then. Minu couldn't wait to get back to the table. He sensed Bella slipping into the next chair, but when he turned around, he was startled to find Katherine.

He choked on his whisky. This triggered a severe paroxysm of coughing that brought tears into his eyes.

Katherine slapped Minu's back to force the liquid out of his windpipe. "Your wife must have thought of you, that's why you choked." Katherine's remark made him smile. He looked around.

"Nobody's stolen her! Your beloved wife is still here." Katherine loved to tease.

Some distance away, Bella was engrossed in conversation. She must have seen him choking, yet she hadn't –

She was chatting animatedly, giggling and laughing so saucily that it was getting on Minu's nerves. Leaving the whisky unfinished, he strode towards Bella. "Shall we leave?"

"So soon?"

Minu could only nod dumbly.

"It's too late for a movie now. Forget it. Enjoy yourself!"

"Shut up!" He wanted to roar. "Let's go!" But the words were stuck in his throat.

"Not to the cinema. I'm not in the mood," he managed, finally. "Let's go home."

"I see." Bella nodded significantly and joined him.

They rode back in silence. Minu hadn't wanted to create a scene in public, but he would definitely let her have it once they got home! I had encouraged her to drink in Bangalore in order to get her into a tender mood, he fumed. How could I imagine that she would flirt around with my own friends? I will not tolerate this!

His anger inflated like a balloon. Bella was silent. She didn't say a word to Minu. Not even to ask him why he was silent.

Minu was seething. She dances with others without even asking me, she doesn't even bother to come to me when I'm choking to death, and now, when I'm silent in anger, she cares two hoots about it!

The balloon had grown very taut.

They entered the house and marched into their bedroom. Minu loosened the knot of his tie and plonked into his chair, without removing his jacket. Bella removed her hairband and had her fingers on the zipper of her gown.

Minu could bear it no longer. Here I am so upset, and yet she can go about her business as if nothing's happened!

The balloon had to explode.

"Bella!" Minu had meant to sound stern, but what came out sounded more like a squawk.

Bella spun around, and strode up to him.

"Minu!" He was contemplating his next words when her strident call assaulted his ears. "I never dreamt that you would stoop so low. Right in front of your wife's eyes! God knows what you would do behind my back! Just as we entered the hall you get hugged and smothered by all those tarts! Couldn't you have chased them away? Then Fulambai brings you a drink, and you gulp it down happily, and force me to drink as well!" She was sizzling with rage. "Agnelo told me what a casanova you were, but let me make it very clear, I will not tolerate it! You're a married man now, your roving days are over. And if you happen to choke, you had better call out to me. Ask any stray Kathy to stroke your back in future – I'll break her back and limbs too!"

Bella's balloon exploded, while the air in Minu's fizzled away. He slumped onto the bed, deflated.

"Minu, did I bore you last night?" she whispered in his ear the next morning, as he opened his eyes.

Minu pondered the question for some time before replying, "No, sweetheart."

These Are My Children

She had finished watering Angela and Anthony. Now, Rosalina stood with a hosepipe before Abel. The young sapling was maturing into adulthood, ready to bear fruit. She could see tiny nuts clustered at the base of the crown. Her coconut trees.

The tinkle of a cycle bell outside the fence cut through her thoughts. She hurried to the gate, leaving the water running out at Abel's roots.

"Rosalinmai, it's nearly noon and you have not finished watering the plants?" asked Vassu the postman, entering through the gate and leaving his cycle to rest on its side stand.

"I couldn't sleep last night and everything got delayed. I dozed off only at dawn and when I woke it was bright and sunny outside."

She knew it was her son Anthony's even before Vassu had handed over the letter. Thank god! She had so been looking forward to it.

Rosalina had been terribly upset ever since she had received the land acquisition notice.

"So thirsty," Vassu fanned himself with a bunch of letters. "Could you give me a glass of water?"

"Of course. Come and sit in the verandah." Rosalina went in to fetch water. "No wonder you're thirsty. It's so hot and humid today."

I wonder what he's written, she thought as she filled the glass. Must have received my letter. Has he decided to come, or has he written to tell me that he can't make it? She was anxious to read his reply, but her eyesight was growing weak these days. And even if she did manage to read, she found it difficult to understand some of the English words. As long as Diniz had been around, she had not needed anybody's help. Two years ago, her husband had died of a sudden heart attack, and now she was forced to rely on others to read her letters.

Why not ask the postman to read the letter, she thought as she came out with the glass of water. Joaquim, her neighbour, would return home only in the evening, by which time her anxiety would have become unbearable.

"Here baba, here's your water." Handing him the tumbler, Rosalina asked, "If you have the time, would you read the letter and tell me what it says, son?"

"Of course. No secrets, I hope!" he quipped, as he slit the letter open.

Of late, Anthony had started typing out his letters to make it easy for his mother to read them. But Diniz's death had broken her spirit and self-confidence. It took her a long time to read a letter and she still had to take it to Joaquim for confirmation.

"It's from Anthony," announced Vassu. "He writes that he's planning to come home with his wife and children at the end of the month. Abel's written to him that he's engaged to an Australian girl. Both Anthony and Angela will be going to Australia from Kuwait and to Bahrain for the wedding in December. Anthony says he'll give you all the other details when he comes. Shall I read it all out?"

Rosalina struggled to bring her wandering mind to the present, taking in all the news. "It's okay. Thank you, son. God bless you."

Vassu went his way.

Rosalina slumped onto the verandah seat.

So that's that. My last bird, too, is building his own nest. Abel had gone to Australia for a job, and now he's getting married. He'll settle down there. Perhaps he will visit Goa with his family, or perhaps not. No! He will return. Hadn't all three of them come home when Diniz died? Surely they'll come when their mother is gone too.

"Are you in, Rosalinmai?" she heard someone call from outside. "Your tap's still running."

Shrugging off her thoughts, Rosalina rushed out and turned off the tap and rolled up the hose. Mechanically, she entered the house. Rice bubbled on the fire, but she wasn't hungry any more. Let the rice boil on, she would have a watery congee. That would save her the trouble of making curry as well. All she needed now was a piece of pickled mango to go with it. After Diniz's death, curry had receded into the culinary background. And since that accursed land acquisition notice arrived some days ago, her appetite had deserted her too.

When Diniz died, all the children had rushed home – Angela from Bahrain, Anthony from Kuwait, and Abel from Australia, though he couldn't make it in time for the funeral. Angela had stayed on till the month's Mind Mass, but the boys had to return to work. Nevertheless, they had stayed on for two whole weeks.

Before his return, Anthony had remarked, "Heard the news, Mai? A new railway line will be passing by our house. It'll be great then. Board the train here in the morning and you're in Bombay by the evening!"

Angela had found the idea of Abel or Anthony trading their flights for a train ride vastly amusing. She had teased them about it too. Nobody had even imagined then, that this demon of it railway line would intrude right into their own home.

When the clerk from the Land Acquisition Office came to serve the notice, Rosalina hesitated. As long as Diniz was

around, she didn't have to take any decisions. At least one of her children should have been with her, she felt, when the notice came. The clerk had been quick to reassure her, "Lots of people have been sent these notices. Why are you so worried? Yours is only a small strip. Many others have had to give up large areas."

"But what will they do with this land?" Rosalina was confused.

"That's their system. Land is simply acquired on both sides of the proposed line. Why are you bothered? Just sign here."

Hesitantly, Rosalina had signed. She knew nothing then. The penny dropped when Joaquim casually mentioned to her, "It seems that part of your fence and some trees are going to be cut."

"Which part, baba? That man told me that land was just going to be acquired on both sides of the line, and now you're telling me that my fence and trees are to be cut!"

"Once the land is acquired, they're free to do anything with it," was Joaquim's casual remark. "Can you stop them?"

She was filled with apprehension. "Exactly which part of my fence and which trees are going to be cut?"

"The part adjoining our land. Twenty of our coconut trees, that mango tree, a banyan tree and our cowshed too. Your front fence, along with the gate, those coconut trees and all the bougainvillea and other bushes." Joaquim rattled off.

Rosalina's dazed mind was in no state to take in any more.

It was a nightmare. She tossed and turned the whole night long.

The three saplings she had planted in the names of her children had grown into healthy coconut trees. She had lavished those young plants with all the maternal love that couldn't reach her children across the seas. They weren't just like her children. They *were* her very own Angela, Anthony and Abel.

"Don't pour your heart out for them, dear," Diniz would chide. "After all, they're only trees. What if one of them falls in a storm, tomorrow?"

And she would be furious. "Why should the tree fall? If it must, then may it fall on me! If it's ruined, may I be ruined with it!"

Sixteen years ago, her eldest child Angela had returned from school excitedly, brandishing a coconut sapling. "Mai, our MLA was distributing coconut saplings. I got one too! Let's plant it in our yard."

Diniz was home on holiday from Kuwait. It was then that Rosalina had told her husband, "Let's plant this sapling. Angela isn't a child any more - soon she'll grow up, get married and leave for her husband's home. This sapling will remind us of her."

Diniz had planted it with his own hands. And as it turned out, Angela was married even before the tree bore fruit.

Diniz had sent a visa for Anthony while he was still in college, after arranging for a job for him in an American company. It was all too soon for Rosalina. Abel, who was still in school, would be with her, but she would miss Anthony a lot. Not just because he was her first son, or because he would support her in her old age. Anthony had taken after his father – he both resembled him, and was just as dependable.

Rosalina called him to her, just before he left. "Anthony my son, my life will feel a little empty, once you've gone. I shall miss you, but I won't stop you – I know your future is important. But do one thing, won't you? Get me a coconut sapling. It will remind me of you."

Anthony made a special trip to the Benaulim nursery to honour her wish. Rosalina got the sapling planted before he left. Today, it had turned into a robust, yielding tree. Truly like Anthony!

The year that Diniz returned for good from Kuwait, Abel got a lucrative job in an Australian company and left to work on a farm near Sydney.

Rosalina was gripped by mixed feelings at the coincidence of Diniz's return and Abel's departure. As the day of his departure to distant Australia drew closer, Abel fetched a coconut sapling on his own, and planted it by the side of Anthony's. Rosalina hadn't known the depths of his concern for her, and was deeply moved by his gesture.

She was content with her husband's protective presence during their twilight years, but she yearned for her children. When Diniz went on his customary evening stroll, leaving her alone, she would be deluged with memories. Then, she would go to the well, draw a dozen pitchers of water and empty them at the feet of Angela, Anthony and Abel.

And now, are they to be cut? These trees that I nurtured like my own children? What do I live for then, she thought, bewildered and angry. After a sleepless night spent tossing and turning, she got out of bed early and went to Joaquim's house.

"Joaquim, are you sure that my coconut trees are to be cut?"

"That's what I hear. We've been asked to collect the compensation money. They're not taking it for free. The compensation is quite good, it seems."

She was filled with chaotic emotions.

"I don't want their money! How dare they put a price on my trees! Damn them! May they roast in hell!" Cursing them to perdition, she returned home.

Most people collected their compensation money while a few, holding out for a better rate, received it under protest. Even Joaquim's father collected his due. Not Rosalina. She wrote to Anthony to come home urgently. She wasn't sure he would. Of late, her children's eagerness to return to Goa had waned. Angela was involved with her own family, and Anthony was drifting away. Earlier, he would come home every two years, but ever since his marriage seven years ago, his visits had become less frequent. He had met his wife in Kuwait. Her family lived in Bombay, and the wedding had taken place there. Diniz couldn't get leave to come, but Anthony had taken his mother to Bombay for the wedding. His next visit home was three years later, with his wife and son. After that, he had come for his father's funeral with the latest addition,

a baby girl. His own family and work kept him busy.

Now that she had received his letter, Rosalina was sure that he would come home. She was filled with relief at the very thought. Anthony was like his father in many ways, and would take care of everything.

Despite such reassuring thoughts, she couldn't help feeling uneasy and restless. And during those times, she rose early, fixed the hose to the tap and treated Angela, Anthony and Abel with given greater affection.

Ever since Diniz had brought her the hose on the day they got the PWD water connection, the task of watering had become much lighter. The solitude that shrouded her after Diniz's death suffocated her. There was no one to talk to. No one to open her heart to. She would sit beside her children then, hose in hand, and talk to them.

"Remember, Angela, the lavish wedding reception your father gave for you, where drinks flowed just like this water! And Anthony, my dear, just because you're in a foreign country you mustn't forget your home. Remember your father built this house with the sweat of his brow for you, his children. Love your wife and children, but never forget your mother, my son!

"And Abel, my boy! Don't think that I love you less. As my youngest child, you should have been dearest to me. And you are. But you know that I tend to lean on Anthony, and you know why – he is so much like your father, that's all. But I love you just as much!"

Even after baring her heart thus, the hose invariably tended to sprinkle an extra dose of water on Anthony.

Abel's letter came a week after Anthony's. He gave details of his fiancée and enclosed her photograph. You must come for the wedding, he wrote.

Rosalina sighed deeply. Abel would visit Goa as a tourist with his family, some day. She could picture the scene –

> Now, this is the Basilica of Born Jesus!
> That is the famous Calangute Beach.
> Here is the headland of Dona Paula.
> *And this is my mother.*

He might then shoot some photographs and take them back with him for his album.

She sobbed at Abel's trunk that day, babbling for hours, pouring out all her apprehensions.

Almost a month had gone by since Anthony's letter. He was already in Bombay, she was told, and would be home next week.

Rosalina made some mackerel para. Anthony loved dried fish pickle. She arranged to get jackfruit from his favourite tree. The fisherwoman was instructed to bring the best available catch.

That morning, as she was busy cleaning the house in preparation for her son's arrival, the neighbouring children called out to her excitedly. "Mai, Mai, come and see, they've come to cut your trees!"

She stood rooted to the spot for a moment. It was as if somebody had aimed an axe at her head. The next moment, she rushed out. Four labourers were waiting at the fence, axes ready.

As she reached the gate, one of the two officials peering into their files enquired, "Shrimati Rosalina Fernandes – is that you?"

She nodded.

"We have to remove the front side of your fence. Those bushes and these three coconut trees will also be cut. It seems you haven't yet collected ..."

"No!" Rosalina was trembling with fury. "You can't cut these coconut trees. They're mine! You dare not touch them!"

"Ma'am, we are government servants. We have our orders. We have to follow them. It isn't just you. Several others have had their trees cleared today. Look over there, the work has already started. The embankment has to be built here and we have to complete the work today itself. Don't disrupt our work, please. Men, dismantle the fence from here."

Cowed down by his authoritative voice, Rosalina pleaded, "Dismantle the fence, take the land, I don't mind. But don't, for God's sake, please don't cut these trees – I beg of you!" She knelt before the official.

"Don't worry Bai, your trees are really A Class – you'll get the maximum price for them. You can even claim money to rebuild your fence."

She felt her temper rise again. "Mister, aren't you ashamed to put a price on my trees? Would you put a price tag on your children's heads? I'm warning you! Take your labourers and go back. My son will be here in a couple of days. He will deal with you!"

The official was furious. "Look here, we have to finish

this work today. Ours is a time-bound programme. You have no right to stop us."

Meanwhile, the labourers had dismanrled the fence and were standing near the trees. They chose Anthony first. A feverish chill ran up her spine. The axe glistened. She shuddered.

Suddenly, she charged at the labourers with the force of an enraged bull. Caught unawares, they lost their balance and fell flat along with their axes.

The next moment, she was hugging Anthony tightly. "Come on, raise your axes!" she shouted at the top of her voice. "Cur me first, then kill my children!"

The unexpected attack from the old woman took the labourers by surprise. At first, they were embarrassed, then they grew angry. Rosalina clung to Anthony with all her might, and the two labourers simply couldn't prise her arms away from the tree.

A crowd had begun to gather. The official was nervous, but refused to give in. As he couldn't use force against an old woman, he adopted a conciliatory tone.

"Bai, you're obstructing government work – that's a grave offence. I request you once again. Please move away. Let the work proceed."

"No!" By now, Rosalina had found within herself a steely resolve. "I won't move! I don't want your money! Don't you dare touch my trees!" she screamed.

The official tried another tack. "Come on men, leave that tree, cut the other one."

A labourer moved towards the smaller tree. At once,

Rosalina left Anthony and rushed to Abel's rescue. Before anybody could stop her, she had pinned the labourer down.

The official rushed to his aid, angry. "Hey! Hey! You have gone too far! We won't tolerate this any more, I tell you!"

But before he could take another step, Rosalina had shoved him violently to the ground too. "You're out to kill my children. I'll see who has the guts to touch them. I curse your children! May they all die! May you be worm food when you're dead!"

Fortunately,]oaquim's father managed to pull her back in time or Rosalina's kick would have landed on the head of the official struggling to get up.

Enraged, the official scooped up his file and strewn papers, called his labourers and stomped off, muttering, 'I'll teach her a lesson!" The crowd heard him swear as he passed them by. He sat in his jeep and drove away.

"Rosalinbai, you shouldn't have done that," Joaquim's father began. "He's a government official after all. You have a point, but ..."

She cut him short. "Does the government have a right to kill my children? Tell them that they can take my land, even my house, but not my trees. Ask them to spare these trees. These are my children! I need them! Save them - save them, please!" she rambled deliriously.

Within half an hour, a police van arrived. The official, now accompanied by an inspector and two constables, strode up to her. Aware of the crowd which had swelled by now, the inspector addressed her in a conciliatory voice: "Look, you have committed an offence by obstructing and manhandling government servants on duty. But I shall persuade them to withdraw their complaint against you, considering your age and your state of mind." Sensing that the crowd found his words reasonable, he moved towards her, "But promise me that you will not obstruct them. Let them do their work."

She realized that she was cornered. This would be the last stand. Give in now, and everything was lost.

"No!" In a frenzy, she rushed ar Anthony and embraced him tight. "I won't let you cut my trees! Cut me first, then cut my children!"

Realizing that her outburst could lead to an ugly. commotion, the inspector promptly signalled to the constables. Three policemen prised her away from the tree. Lifting her bodily, they carried her to the van.

Joaquim's father, along with some elders, tried to plead with the inspector, but the men carried Rosalina away.

That fateful day, Angela, Anthony and Abel in his first flush of inflorescence, were felled.

The District Collector's office was jammed by a crowd of fifty odd villagers along with the sarpanch, all seeking Rosalina's release. She was finally released around noon and taken home.

Despite her awareness of the fate of her trees, Rosalina blacked out at the stark sight of the fallen trunks.

Thanks to the efforts of her neighbours and the doctors

she regained consciousness the next day. Anthony's letter reached her on the same day.

Dear Mai,

I have been stuck in Bombay for the last one week. I just couldn't make it to Goa, though I wanted to come and see you. I am rushing back to Kuwait as I have received a telex from my office to return. I'll try to come next year. Meanwhile, don't fret over the land acquisition and those trees. I'll send you all the money you need. Please take care of yourself.

Your loving son,
Anthony.

She shut her eyes, praying for them to remain closed forever.

Chastity Belt

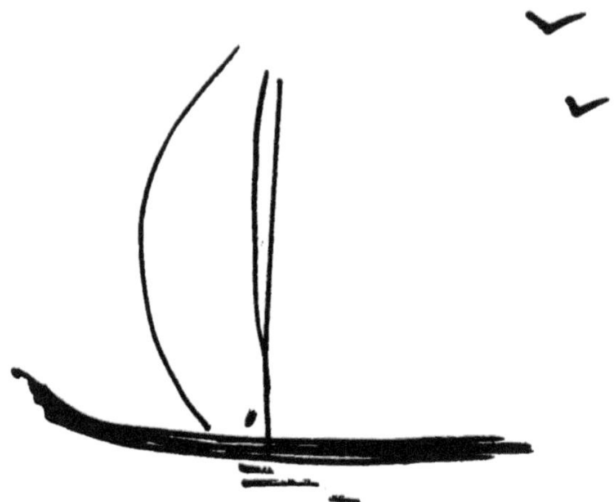

The Customs Officer rummaged through Michael's luggage. Digging out a calculator, he tossed it into his drawer. One of the two vials of perfume followed.

Michael had splurged on a beautiful designer watch for Rosy and had often dreamt of it on her delicate wrist during the voyage. He was overcome with dismay as he saw the officer lay his eager hands on it. "Sahib! Meri biwi ke liye laya –"

"Then why did you bring just

one?" came the brutal retort. "What about my wife? She wants one too!"

Any argument in the face of such obvious arrogance would only mean the slapping of a heavy duty, and so Michael kept quiet. Fortunately, the dinner set was ignored. Silently praying for the stereo to get through, he saw the avaricious official grabbing the orange sari, the best of the three he had bought Rosy. Michael clenched his teeth tight. Not that all this let him off lightly – he still had to fork out a hefty duty.

Damn these Customs bastards, he fumed in cold fury as he walked out of the enclosure. His shipmates who had been cleared had flocked around the company agent, who had come with their payroll. Michael walked out of the docks, his pockets heavy with the accumulated wages of his nine-month voyage.

Michael shared a cab with Peter, heading towards Dhobi Talao where most Goan kudds or village clubs were located. As they halted at a traffic signal, his eyes fell on a family planning hoarding, depicting the ideal family of four – "Hum do hamare do". The father's face resembled Michael's, more or less, but the mother's face was not a patch on Rosy's.

Rosy. It was over nine months since he had last seen her. He suddenly recalled Rosy's letter, which the company agent had given him along with the wages. He now pulled it out of his pocket.

Their son was two months old, she had written, and not yet baptized. They were all waiting for Michael. All?

Whom did Rosy mean by All? Mother? Sisters? Friends and neighbours? It didn't matter to him; it was Rosy who was waiting. The last time too, when their first child was born, she had waited two months to christen the girl, he recalled. Despite everybody's disapproval of the delay, Rosy had wanted Michael to be there. When he finally arrived, they had had a solemn baptism ceremony at the church followed by a litany and a grand party at home.

Memories of her face never failed to light up Michael's face during the voyage. Now his face brightened again at the thought of Rosy waiting for him for the naming ceremony of the child. Christening? Just a pretext! Rosy must be longing for him!

Their son resembled him a lot, she had written. He recalled old Salvador's words, "When a pregnant woman is deeply in love with her husband and thinks of him day and night, the child invariably takes after the father." Rosy had definitely been thinking of him all the time, pregnant or otherwise!

"What are you thinking of, man?" Peter cut into his thoughts.

Michael felt like confiding in someone, but remembered that it had been this very Peter who had once ridiculed him. While on the subject of marriage and fidelity, Michael had once remarked that an ideal wife should be like Rosy, especially for a sailor, and Peter had guffawed, saying, "Every seaman believes that his wife is a faithful angel!" His sneering comment had irritated

Michael a good deal, but realizing that an argument would lead from one thing to another, he had kept quiet.

Rosy may not be an angel, but there was never any doubt of her faithfulness to him.

But there were also wives like Carmina!

Michael's thoughts wandered over to his youth.

He had been at a loose end after failing his SSCE. Aiyee wanted him to hunt for a job, while his father wanted him to appear again for the High School exam. But his heart tugged at a third option - the life of a sailor. Not out of any love for ships or the sea, but for those fat salaries. His adolescent eyes would regard the obvious prosperity of the village seamen with reverence. Those flashy golddrimmed Raybans, thick gold chains coruscating through their stylishly half-buttoned shins, fingers weighed down by numerous thick gold rings and wrists brandishing new foreign watches!

His friendship with Caitan was a result of the desire to fulfil this ambition. Finding him in a good mood one day, Michael had confided his ambition of joining the merchant navy. Caitu, who had a good friend at the recruiting office in Bombay, had promised him that by his next trip, he would have a sea job ready for Michael.

When Caitu went back to sea, Michael continued to visit Caitu's family. He had to remain in the man's good books, after all. Carmina, his wife, was often requested to remind Caitan of his assurance to Michael in her letters.

He vividly remembered the day he was returning from

the village market when he bumped into Carmina. "Hi Michael! Going home? C'mon, give me a lift!"

She had hopped onto the crossbar of his bicycle without waiting for a reply. She had gained some weight in two years of marriage; Michael had to pedal hard.

"So ... !" she began. "What are you doing this evening?"

"Nothing." He was idle, after all, and had plenty of time on his hands.

"There's a bag of rice to be brought from Margao. Will you come with me to town?"

"Sure."

"Mai," she called out to her mother-in-law, as she got down from his bike. "Mai, I'm taking Michael with me to bring rice from Margao. Those shopkeepers are cheats and the coolies fleece you. Michael will be a great help, I'm sure."

The old lady agreed, for she trusted Michael's common sense. "Choose good, old rice, Michael," she advised.

It was not yet three when they reached Margao, and the shops were still closed.

"Michael, what movie is showing at Metropole?"

"No idea."

"Haven't you seen any movie recently?"

"No. I don't go very often." He preferred the Tiatr, the local Konkani theatre.

"Shall we watch a movie? We'll go to the market later."

And he had nodded.

She kept whispering to him all through the movie, tugging at his arm. And he had been acutely embarrassed when, a couple of times, his elbow brushed against her breasts.

It was late evening when they returned home.

"The rice wasn't good enough," he lied to Mai. "They expect better quality stuff next week." Their secret lay buried within themselves.

Many movies later, Carmina had furtively called him over to her room. Making sure that her mother-in-law was asleep, she had made him enter through the window. Michael chose to ignore the disparity in their ages as he allowed himself to be seduced by the older woman. That was his first experience of love or rather, of sex.

He felt a wave of disgust wash over him now as memories of Carmina intruded into his thoughts of Rosy.

Slamming the door of the cab that had stopped beyond Metro Cinema, Michael alighted along with Peter. They crossed the road and climbed the stairs to their club. Leaving his bags to be stowed in place by his friend, he walked across to the office of Goa Travels and back.

"Got your ticket?" asked Peter.

"Yes."

He lay down but could not sleep a wink.

Peter was dressing up to go out. Michael, however, wasn't in the mood for it.

"Coming for a movie, Michael?"

"Where? Metro?"

"No, I'm going to see a Hindi picture today."

It had been a long time. Yes, nine long months since they had last seen a movie.

Abruptly, Michael changed his mind. "Okay, let's go."

They went out into the street. The bustling crowds, the broad streets, the skyscrapers, swanky hotels and posh shopping arcades – everything reminded him of Rosy. She hadn't been to Bombay yet. She had been eager to see it, and Michael had wanted to bring her here and show off the big city's attractions to her. They had even planned for her to come to see him off, on two previous occasions. But then, both trips had had to be put off because she had been in the early stages of pregnancy then and was not allowed to travel.

I must make a special trip to Bombay for a whole week with Rosy this time, he decided. Eight whole days alone with her! The prospect itself was thrilling.

He remembered the early days of their marriage, a period of ecstatic pleasure. He had postponed marriage until the age of thirty two, afraid that he would be saddled with a wife like Carmina. Those lost years spent avoiding marriage had been more than made up in the whirlwind of those two months.

A sailor's wife is the target of ridicule for the idle and the chauvinistic the world over. Michael needed no further proof, for he had himself tasted the pudding!

It was this bitter truth that had made him dread marriage. The thought of leaving his wife behind and going abroad was an absolute nightmare.

He had of course been too raw to have harboured any such forebodings during his liaison with Carmina.

Caitu had kept his promise and sent Michael his papers. Michael recalled the last night he had spent with Carmina, before embarking on his first trip. "Will you miss me?" he had asked in between their lovemaking.

"Why? Won't I get someone else?" was the tart response. He had thought then that she had been joking.

When he returned from his first voyage though, he discovered that she had already found another paramour. It dawned on him then that some people could keep love and lust in two separate compartments.

Memories of Rosy, aroused by all the romancing in the Hindi movie at the Liberty, added to his discomfort. Rosy should have been there with him. When he took her to the cinema, he wanted no one else with them. Unbidden, thoughts of Carmina returned, reminding him especially of the time he had gone along with Caitu and Carmina to a movie. Caitu had put his arm around her shoulder, tickling and petting her. Pretending to ignore them, he had tried to concentrate on the screen, but had ended up becoming highly aroused – probably even more than Caitu.

Michael boarded the Goa-bound bus the next afternoon. The bus was stopped at the Panvel octroi-naka, where his conspicuously foreign suitcase was brought down for checking, and promptly returned after the mandatory hundred rupee note had exchanged hands.

Thrice, his sleep was disturbed that night, and all three times, Rosy flitted through his dreams.

Early next morning, as the bus left Sawantwadi, a fellow passenger started gathering his baggage.

"Getting down at Assonora?" Michael inquired.

"No," the elderly man smiled, embarrassed. "I know it's childish. I come home from Bombay every year. Once the bus crosses Sawantwadi, I get the feeling that I'm almost home and start gathering my luggage! And then I get impatient because we just don't seem to get there."

Michael agreed wholeheartedly. He too, often felt the same way. The old man continued, "Usually, we find the journey from Margao to Bicholim long and tedious, but when we're coming from Bombay, we cross the Maharashtra border and get the feeling that we're about to reach Margao."

Michael nodded, but he had lost interest in the conversation by now. Anxiety to reach home had made him restive ever since the ship had dropped anchor outside Bombay harbour and waited three days to get docked. Those three days never seemed to end. Then the unloading, the Customs clearance, the ride to the club, the boarding of the bus, and now at last in Goa – his home a mere fingertip away.

At eight in the morning, when the bus stopped at Panjim to drop off some passengers, an impatient Michael shouted at the conductor, "Why're you waiting? We're already late!"

"Arre baba, you're lucky," the conductor pacified him. "Normally we reach Panjim only at nine, sometimes even at ten."

Margao at last! He jumped into the first available taxi and hurried home.

Rosy must have been nursing the child, for she rushed out with the baby still at her breast when she heard Michael coming. A reunion after nine months! Michael embraced her tightly.

"Arre, arre! Don't squash Baba! Look at him, at least!"

The baby! He looks just like me! Michael hugged Rosy again, remembering old Salvador's words. "You were thinking of me day and night, no?" he whispered in her ears, unmindful of Mai. "That's why he looks so much like me!"

Then he hugged his mother.

He didn't step out for the next four days. He and Rosy sat together, ate together and slept together; there was so much to share.

This was how it had been when they were newly married. Three months had sped by and Michael was least concerned about going back to the sea. Each time he received a call, he simply sent back a medical certificate.

Even Rosy had asked him once, "When do you plan to leave?"

"You want me to?"

"It isn't that. But people are talking. And Mai keeps asking me – she even asked you the other day, didn't she?"

"Let them talk." he had retorted. "Why does it bother you?"

"You don't understand, Michael. Everyone says that you're still smitten by your wife!"

Smitten he certainly was! And why not? Her beautiful face complemented her perfect figure, which was what had prompted him to marry her. But what if she turned into another Carmina if he left her and went to sea?

Michael had often justified Carmina's infidelity to himself with the logic that the blame lay with husbands who left their young wives at home, starved of love. How long was a woman expected to deny her body?

Now, however, his sentiments had taken a different turn. What had begun as a niggling worry turned into an obsession. Rosy couldn't be taken on the ship with him, and leaving her at home would attract the lascivious glances of the village louts. Mai was growing older by the day. Rosy was certainly blameless, but anyone could fall prey to temptation.

He had even considered giving up his sea job, but the good news had come suddenly – Rosy was pregnant.

Free of his marital worries at last, he had asked his mother to take good care of Rosy, and buoyantly resumed his duties.

"Michael," Rosy had asked then, "won't you be here when our son is born?"

He had hugged her tightly. "You know that the trip takes nine months. I won't wait a day longer, I promise."

She had swallowed her disappointment. "But you know that I'll wait to baptize the child, don't you? This is my second month. Baba will be two months old when you return. But I'll wait."

And she had, indeed, waited. Only, that first time, it was a daughter.

The next time had been a re-enactment of the first episode. Michael's days flew in Rosy's company, after their reunion. Weeks blurred into months. Calls were fended off by medical certificates. Tongues began wagging once again, and Mai fretted about the ignored call letters.

Then, once again – good news!

"Let's hope it's a boy this time." Rosy had whispered in his ear.

"We'll pray for a son," Michael had whispered back. His ship had been in Genoa, seven months later, when he received the news. Michael had danced on hearing that he had had a son, and had felt an intense longing to return home. He had even toyed with the idea of going back on medical grounds. But it had only been two months, and he had given up the idea regretfully. A departure then would have meant a blot on his career record.

And now at last, he was home. Days flew by in Rosy's company.

"I'd better give up sea life," he quipped one evening. "I think I'll resign."

Her reply was blunt. "Are you mad Michael? What sort of job will you get here?"

This was quite true. But, it was equally true that even after two children, Rosy was still as beautiful as ever. Smooth and supple, her body had not a hint of flab anywhere. She still aroused him as sensually as she had on their wedding night. Her body hadn't lost its battle with age as other women's did, after the first pregnancy. Some became thin and haggard, while others bloated up like pumpkins. They couldn't think of attracting even a squint-eyed glance! No doubt it saved their husbands any anxiety about their infidelity.

But a young woman like Rosy. Slim and youthful. What could he do? There was no solution in sight.

"We're lucky to have a boy and a girl," she murmured to him, as they lay together in bed. "Should we put a stop?"

Suddenly, Michael was attentive. "Huh? Why?"

"Two's enough. A small family is good in all respects. Any more pregnancies will ruin my figure."

He cut her short. The computer in his brain whirred and out popped the answer he was frantically looking for.

It didn't matter if her figure would be ruined. No lascivious eye would follow her! No covetous glance follows a woman during pregnancy and a few months thereafter. This period is the safest to go on a voyage and return in time, to begin the safety measures all over again.

"Don't worry about the children." Michael declared decisively. "That's my responsibility."

Two months later, he embarked on another ship, yet again. Free of worry.

Damodar Mauzo

Eminent Konkani writer Damodar Mauzo received the Sahitya Akademi Award for his novel *Karmelin* in 1983. He has also won the Goa Kala Academy Award, the Konkani Bhasha MandaI Award and the Janaganga Award. In 1997 he was awarded the Best Dialogue Award at the Goa Film Festival for the film *Shitoo*, and the Best Screenplay Award at the Goa State Film Festival in 2005 for *Aleesha*. His works have been translated into many Indian languages as well as into French. He participated actively in the Konkani Porjecho Avaz movement that successfully culminated in achieving official language status for Konkani.

XavierCota

Xavier Cota is a social activist and convenor of Betalbatim Civic and Consumer Forum, an N GO working in the field of consumer activism and civic rights awareness in Goa. He translates from Konkani and Portuguese to English, and has received the Katha Award for Translation for Mahabaleshwar Sail's Konkani story "Monisbuddi".

S P Chendvanker

Born in Mumbai in 1947, S P Chendvanker studied at the J J School of Art. Presently a lecturer at the Goa College of Art, Chendvanker's work is a reflection of his daily routine and his spirituality. He has received awards from the Art Society in Mumbai, the Kala Academy in Goa and the Indian Academy of Fine Art in Amritsar.

doctor, engineer, policewoman, mechanic, computer specialist...

What will I be?

What happens when 1,300 children, a determined Katha team of teachers and activists, and a whole community come together? Yes ... Sheer magic! You'll find this excitement in the air when you enter our school, a low-cost brick building.

We, the children and women of Govindpuri, a large slum cluster of more than 1,50,000 people, have come a long way in more than fourteen years with Katha. But there are excitements ahead. Small but sure steps towards self-confidence, self-reliance touched by the power of self-esteem. Many of us are working today to support our families in ways we could never have dreamt of. Many of us have finished our BAs and BComs from Delhi colleges. Once, we didn't dare to dream. Today, seeing our dreams come true, we talk of what Katha's goal of an uncommon education for a common good can help us all achieve. We are fun-loving dreamers-doers at Katha. And we'd like you to join us in our fight against poverty.

Be our special friend! Sponsor quality education at Katha. Giving has never been so easy, and with so much impact. It costs you just Rs 250/month to provide basic quality education to one of us. That's Rs 3,000/yr. Include computer education for a child with just Rs 1,800/yr more!

Please send your cheque/DD in favour of Katha Resources to Educate a Child (REACH) Fund to **Katha, A3, Sarvodaya Enclave, Sri Aurobindo Marg, New Delhi 110017**. For more details visit us at **www.katha.org**. Or write to us at **networking@katha.org**.

Donations to Katha Reach Fund qualify for 100% tax exemption under 35 AC of the IT Act. Registered under FCRA, Katha can receive donations in foreign currencies.

Thank you for buying this Katha book.

10% of its jacket price goes to Katha's programme for educating children living on the streets or in the slum clusters of Delhi, or in Changlang district in Arunachal Pradesh. The 17 Katha schools include three Tamasha Schools on Wheels. Katha has been working with communities, and especially children and women, since 1990. For more information on our poverty alleviation programmes, please visit us at www.katha.org

www.ingramcontent.com/pod-product-compliance
Ingram Content Group UK Ltd.
Pitfield, Milton Keynes, MK11 3LW, UK
UKHW041824200726
13854UKWH00002BA/541